Cleansed by Fire

A Father Frank Mystery

James R. Callan

*To Mary!
Enjoy the read.
James R Callan*

Pennant Publishing

This is a work of fiction. All names, characters, places, and events are the work of the author's imagination. Any resemblance to real persons, places, or events is coincidental.

Cleansed by Fire
Copyright: James R. Callan ©2012

Cover Art: Evan Scheidegger

ISBN-13:   978-0-9646850-6-2
ISBN-10:   0-9646850-6-X

www.pennant-publishing.com

Printed in the united States of America

Pennant Publishing

This book is dedicated to Earlene, who has been very supportive throughout the long and arduous process of writing this and other books.

~ CHAPTER ONE ~

"**B**less me Father for I have sinned."

Father Frank DeLuca waited in the dark behind the screen of the Prince of Peace confessional. The voice sounded familiar, like he should know the person but he quickly wiped that thought from his mind. He did not want to know who it was.

When nothing more came, he said, "How long has it been since you last took the Sacrament of Reconciliation?"

"Ah, I don't remember. Kind of a long time."

"Is there something in particular that has brought you back today?"

Another silence.

Finally, "I knew about the fire Thursday."

Thursday. Father Frank's mind searched through the events of two days ago.

"You mean the Pine Valley Baptist Church? That fire?"

"Yes, Father." Then he quickly added, "I didn't set it or nothin'."

When the boy did not continue, Father Frank said, "But ...?"

"I knew it was going to happen. And I didn't tell nobody, uh, anybody. I mean, I didn't tell the police."

Father Frank furrowed his eyebrows and ran a hand through his black, curly hair. He hadn't heard if the fire had been classified as arson or an accident.

"Do you mean you knew someone was going to set fire to the church before it happened?"

"Yes."

Father Frank's mind raced down several paths at once. As a rule, the priest tried not to recognize any penitent. Tonight, with news of the arson, his mind inadvertently associated the voice with a name—Sammie Winters. Did someone tell the boy they were going to burn a church? Did he have a vision or premonition? Sammie didn't seem the type. Had he heard someone talking about it?

"How do you know this?"

The teenager remained quiet for a moment before answering, almost in a whisper.

"I, uh, I heard someone say they were going to burn a church."

"Why didn't you tell the authorities?"

"I couldn't. Uh—you don't understand. I just couldn't."

The priest closed his eyes and rested his forehead in his hands, suddenly weary. Could the fire have been prevented? He took a deep breath. He was supposed to give guidance. He raised his head.

"You're right, I don't understand. But God will. Talk to Him. Tell him you're sorry for your sins, and say a Rosary for the people who lost their church."

"Yes, Father."

"I absolve you from all your sins." Father Frank made a sign of the cross. "In the name of the Father, the Son, and the Holy Spirit."

The priest cleared his throat. "There is one other thing. Since you know who committed the crime, you really should tell the police. Now. If you don't, this is going to weigh on you like a lead warm-up jacket. You have information that can help the police solve a crime. You have an obligation to tell them."

The boy said nothing but Father Frank heard the door open and close. Sammie was gone.

The priest sat in the darkness, eyes wide open, as he hoped no one else came into the confessional tonight. Sammie Winters knew Pine Valley Baptist had been arson. He probably also knew the name of the arsonist. Why wouldn't he tell the police?

The priest sighed. Maybe Sammie was more involved than he indicated. Maybe he pushed someone into setting the fire. What *was* the extent of his participation?

Sammie didn't seem like the type to be involved in serious crime. He seemed like a good kid, and attended mass every Sunday with his parents. Yet, some connection existed between Sammie and the arson. Father Frank shook his head. Maybe he didn't know Sammie that well since he wasn't involved in any church activities. Nice looking kid, about fifteen. What had he gotten himself into?

Even now Father Frank could see the inferno—red and orange flames with yellow tongues flickering, roaring, stretching upward, trying to reach the tall pine trees that towered over the white frame church. He could feel the heat, pulsing on the breeze.

First hot, then warm, then hot again, lest you forget it was consuming a building. He could hear the frustration of those trying to save something—firemen who were losing the battle, parishioners who were losing their church, and Reverend Fisher, wringing his hands, almost in tears. Just a month ago, he had celebrated his twentieth year as the minister of Pine Valley Baptist.

The church burned to the ground.

At least no one was killed. Allan Moore, one of the volunteer firefighters, had sustained serious burns when he tripped and fell on live coals. Maybe all of that could have been avoided if Sammie had told the police what he had known before the fire was set. Father Frank said a quick prayer that Pine Valley Baptist would rebound, rebuild, and use this misfortune to draw closer to God. And the priest prayed that Sammie would go to the police and tell what he knew.

Father Frank guessed the crowd of gawkers to be over fifty. He'd been there too, watching the firemen struggle to put out the fire and work to see it didn't spread to adjoining properties. He had felt a deep loss, watching a house of God being destroyed, not knowing what he could do.

He felt the same way now. What could he do? He shook his head in the solitude of the confessional. Nothing. The seal of confession prevented him from telling anybody, even the police, what he had heard from Sammie.

And yet, how could he do nothing? Someone had destroyed a church. Not his church but a Christian church, and that was like a cousin being attacked.

~ Chapter Two ~

"**G**eorgia," Father Frank called out. "Got a minute?"

The thirty-three-year-old priest had just finished Monday morning mass, and Georgia Peitz, one of the most faithful attendees to weekday masses, was walking out the door.

As usual, she looked crisp and fresh, unaffected by the heat or humidity. Today she wore a sea-green dress that complemented her emerald eyes and highlighted her trim figure. The light, southerly breeze ruffled her auburn hair, shaped in a Princess Diana cut. She turned, nodded, and came up the aisle to meet him.

"Good morning, Father. How is everything?" she asked.

"Good. But things can usually be better." His dark eyes twinkled. "That's where you come in."

"I'm not teaching this summer. I have some time."

Father Frank laughed. "You always have time to help out, no matter how busy you are." He turned serious. "You know about the POPsters?"

She nodded.

By now, everybody in the parish knew about the teen choir he was trying to get started. He'd mentioned it at church several times, had made a plea to any teenagers who liked to sing, and even held a contest to select a name for the group.

Over a dozen names were entered, including The Choristers, The Gregorians (after St. Gregory, the patron saint of choirs), the Songsters, and the POPsters (with Prince of Peace providing the POP). When Father Frank put it to a vote of those who showed up for the first meeting of the choir, POPsters won.

"Phyllis Traynor has taken on the task of running it," said Father Frank.

A small smile crept over Georgia's face.

Father Frank took a deep breath and let it out slowly. "She's a love. The easiest person in the world to work with. And eager."

"I sense a *but* coming," said Georgia.

"How do I put this?"

Georgia said it for him. "Phyllis is not the most organized person in the world, right? And you think I might be able to keep her on track."

"I do." Father Frank sighed in relief. "And I would be eternally grateful if you could approach her and offer to help."

"You haven't said anything to her?"

"Heavens, no. I wouldn't risk hurting her feelings. She's such a sweet, sincere person. But if you just offered to help, it would be really good for the POPsters.

"I want this youth choir to do well. We have few enough activities for the teens in Pine Tree."

"Your Street Three basketball league, or whatever you call it, is getting a lot of interest. I hear it's open to all the teens in town."

Father Frank's serious expression dissolved into a wide smile. "Three on Three Summer B-Ball, and it is. The main thing is to provide some wholesome activities for all of the city's youth, not just those at Prince of Peace. Besides, it's a lot more fun for everybody if there are more kids involved. And you know how close basketball is to my heart."

He placed his right hand over his heart, and grinned. "However, a lot of teens aren't into sports. The POPsters provide another outlet for them. And anybody can join. See what you can do?"

"Sounds like fun to me. Phyllis and I get along well. I'll *accidentally* bump into her today. And I'll put the POPsters on my prayer List."

"Excellent."

She fished a piece of paper out of her pocket. "I have a list of people I want to remember in prayers every day. The POPsters are made up of people." Her mouth curved into a silly grin. "So it'll fit."

He wrinkled his forehead. "On paper?"

"Of course. Wouldn't be fair to forget anybody, now would it?"

"Okay, guys. Here are the results from the first round of play." Father Frank attached a large poster to the fence surrounding the basketball court at City Park.

Forty-two teenaged boys jockeyed for position to see where their teams stood in the rankings.

"As I'm sure you all remember from the start of Three on Three Summer B-Ball, if any team wins too much, we split it up for the next round of play. The Jaguars went undefeated, and the Impalas lost only one game.

"So, I've taken the six guys from those two teams, and paired each with two guys from the bottom four teams."

Six of the boys started grumbling.

"Come on Father."

"That's not fair."

"How come we gotta break up?"

Father Frank held up both hands, palms toward the crowd. "Guys, we agreed it would be more fun if it were competitive. It's no fun, for either side, if you know who's going to win before you start."

"How 'bout taking just one guy off the Jags?" asked a slender kid who matched Father Frank's six foot height, but weighed twenty pounds less than the priest's one-seventy-five.

"Yeah." Father Frank chuckled. "And the new guy never sees the ball. We agreed it was not about winning but having fun. We'll run it this way for the next round, rebalance, and finish with the third round in August. Then we'll see how each of you did individually while playing with different guys."

"How 'bout the Bears?" asked Carlos, a chunky kid with Latino blood in his background. "They're good and they get to stay together."

"You're right. They were ten and three. And if they're on top in the second round, they'll get split for the last round." Father Frank scanned the group. "It *will* work, guys. Just give it a chance."

The grumbling subsided, if not the disappointment on the faces of the two winning teams.

Father Frank nodded. "Okay. Here are the new teams and the schedule. Play starts tomorrow. Get in a little practice. First game is at ten."

A black Trans-Am with tinted windows cruised by slowly, made a U-turn and drove back by the playground. Father Frank followed the car with his eyes for a moment.

"Any of you guys know who that is?"

Most of the boys were silent, some shook their heads. A few said *no* but none of them looked at the priest, and he felt certain at least some of them were not telling the truth.

"Okay, guys. See you tomorrow."

Father Frank turned in time to see the Trans-Am disappear around the corner. He'd seen it several times, crawling along, looking for someone or something. Father Frank felt certain the driver and car were not from Pine Tree. Not that he knew every car in this town of eighteen thousand. An itch at the base of his skull told him the driver was not a positive addition to the community.

If he'd been looking for something, why not stop, roll down the window and ask? Father Frank knew that wasn't the case. That car had been skulking around for a week. Besides, dark tinted windows always bothered Father Frank. Dark windows masked dark thoughts, unless you were a movie star and it was the only way you could get any privacy.

Probably connected with drugs, Father Frank thought. *That's the biggest problem today. No. Not true. The biggest problem is people drifting away from God. From church. Fix that and the drug problem would go away. Of course, drugs are part of the cause of people turning their backs on God. Vicious cycle.*

Father Frank brought his attention back to the basketball court. Some of the kids continued to study the schedule, others drifted off, and still others discussed practice times.

Sammie Winters wasn't here, and hadn't shown any interest in the basketball league. That was all right. Basketball didn't appeal to everyone, although Father Frank couldn't understand why not.

Frank loved the game, had since grade school. He'd led the Jesuit Prep team in both scoring and assists his senior year. A basketball scholarship had taken him to the University of Texas at Arlington, and by his second season, he had earned a starting position as point guard.

The summer following his sophomore year he felt an irresistible call to the priesthood. After many long conversations with Monsignor Decker, a chaplain on campus, Frank entered Holy Trinity Seminary located on the University of Dallas campus. He had never regretted that move but he did miss competitive basketball.

Father Frank reached the parish's seven-year-old, maroon Taurus with its crumpled right-rear fender, courtesy of a telephone pole that was surely in the wrong place. He patted the fender.

"You have to wait. If we get a good collection Sunday, the parish might spring for new tires. These are as bald as my dad's head."

Georgia watched Phyllis Traynor get out of her car and try to lock it when all the materials she tried to balance slipped from her arms and scattered over the drive. She groaned as she bent to pick them up, and Georgia guessed it was out of frustration.

"Here, let me help you with those. Looks like you've got your hands full."

Georgia Peitz stooped and began to scoop up song booklets, paper cups, and napkins, while Phyllis pushed several large bottles of soda back into a plastic bag.

"Thanks, Georgia. I guess I shouldn't try to carry everything at once."

"I do the same thing all the time." She straightened up. "I'll carry some of this stuff."

Inside the parish hall, Phyllis put the bag of drinks on a table. "I really do appreciate it. The kids will be here any minute and I still need to arrange the room."

"Would you like some help?"

Phyllis sighed. "Thank you. I accept. I hardly know where to start."

"If you'd like, I'll set up the snack table and get the drinks ready, while you handle the booklets and chairs. Is that what you had in mind?"

Without waiting for an answer, Georgia began to arrange drinks on the table.

"Sounds good to me," said Phyllis and she began lining up the chairs in two rows, while putting a song booklet on each.

A few minutes later, the kids began arriving, and by ten after seven, eighteen girls and four boys milled around the room.

"Should you get started?" Georgia whispered to Phyllis. "The natives are getting restless."

"I guess so." Phyllis glanced at the door. "Usually, I wait 'til Roger gets here but he's late tonight."

"Start them on something. You want them to know it starts on time, so they'll plan to be here on time."

Phyllis called the group to order and asked them to sing, *The Battle Hymn of the Republic*, from page nine in the song booklet. In the middle of the song, Roger walked in, surveyed the room, and joined Georgia at the snack table.

At the end, Phyllis looked over and waved to her husband. He acknowledged her, and then said to the kids,

"How many of you guys know *Yakety Yak*?"

Some hands went up, and other kids called out, "Right on," "Yeah," "All right," and "Great song."

Phyllis wrinkled her forehead. "Uh, I don't know it."

One of the girls in the front row said, "We do. Just give us a start cue."

Phyllis shrugged and said, "One, two, three."

The kids started a little hesitantly but by the second verse, they were into it with full teenage enthusiasm.

"Just finish cleaning up your room.
Let's see that dust fly with that broom.
Get all that garbage out of sight,
Or you don't go out Friday night.
Yakety, yak (don't talk back).
Yakety yak. Yakety yak."

When they finished, spontaneous cheers rang out, hands stabbed the air, there were high-fives, and every face sported a huge grin.

"How 'bout *Wake Me Up When September Ends*," one of the boys said.

Phyllis turned and looked at Georgia and Roger. Uncertainty painted her face.

Roger stood. "How about a good, rousing version of *Holy God We Praise Thy Name* first, and then we can do *Wake Me Up When September Ends*. How's that sound?"

"Cool."

"That's page four in your booklets," Phyllis said.

At the conclusion of the hymn, Roger stood again. "Before we go on to *Wake Me Up When September Ends*, how about we try *Holy God* again, and this time, we add a little harmonizing. We'll do something simple, like, the guys can take the bass line."

"We don't know how to do that stuff," one of the boys called out.

"Okay," said Roger. "Let me plunk this out on the piano, so you can hear the harmony line." He went to the old upright piano. "First, here's the melody." He tapped a few keys. "Now, this is what the bass will sound like."

Again he laid his hands on the keyboard and played a few notes.

"Hear that? Let me play it one more time. Listen closely." After a few notes, Roger asked, "Well, what do you think?"

"I don't know," said one of the boys.

"Tell you what. I'll stand in the middle of you guys so you can follow me. How's that sound?"

"I don't know," said the same boy.

"We won't know until we try. Let's give it a whirl."

With that, Roger moved over, stood with the boys, and nodded to his wife.

After the song, Roger asked, "What do you think, guys?"

"We weren't too bad," a boy with a blond ponytail said.

A petite brunette, with her own ponytail, turned toward the back row where the boys stood.

"You were bad, and I don't mean good bad."

"Oh yeah? Think you could do any better?"

"I don't think. I *know*."

"Okay, guys," Roger jumped in. "Before this comes to blows, here's a possibility. If, and only if, you want to try it, we could split the girls up into sopranos and altos. We let the boys be the bass. Then we could do some real harmony. What do you think?"

Eyebrows went up, shoulders slumped, frowns appeared, and a few eyes opened very wide.

"What if we can't do it?" asked a slightly plump girl with copper-colored hair.

"If we—you—decide you can't do it, then we'll stop. Simple as that. We give it a try. If it works, great. And I think you'll really enjoy it. If it doesn't work, no harm done. We give it up."

"I say let's go for it," said the brunette who had challenged the boys.

"We've done it already," said the boy with the ponytail. "If you girls aren't too chicken, let's do it."

The girl raised her chin, gave him a very superior look, and flipped *her* ponytail as she snapped back toward Roger.

"We're in. Right, girls?"

~ Chapter Three ~

The lock yielded in less than five seconds. He picked up the plastic container, slipped inside and eased the door closed. He stood motionless, his eyes adjusting to the darkness, his ears searching for any sound that might indicate danger. He smirked. *I am the danger.*

Faint light filtered through the dark windows on one side of the building. He shifted his stance and his shoe scraped the floor. His head jerked, startled by how loud it seemed in the complete silence that engulfed him. He held his breath, straining to see or hear anything he might have disturbed.

The quiet and darkness remained unchanged. Too bad for anyone who came in now. The church would burn tonight. It would crash down into ashes. Crash to ashes. He liked the sound of that.

Bad break, building. Not your fault. But it's gotta happen.

His eyes had adjusted to the minimal light. Shapes and features of the building came into focus. He could make out the pews, gauge the length of the aisle, and see the pulpit.

Time to get to work, take care of business.

He walked deeper into the darkness, stepping carefully, trying to make as little noise as possible. About halfway down the aisle, he stopped and unscrewed the top from the container he carried. He began splashing the pungent liquid on the floor, as he backed toward the door he had entered.

When he finished, he screwed the lid back on, and set the can on the floor near the entrance. Carefully, he cracked the door and peered out, scanning the area, making sure no one had driven up. All clear. He eased the door closed.

He pulled a piece of paper out of his pocket, rolled it into a thin tube about the size of a drinking straw, then gave it a twist in the middle to hold it together. He fished a match from his shirt pocket, struck it and lit the paper.

For a moment, he watched the flame crawl along the napkin, creating shadows that danced on the floor. When most of the paper tube was aflame, he tossed it on the floor a few feet in front of him. With amazing speed, the diesel caught and exploded to life.

He stepped back and watched as the fire spread, his eyes reflecting the growing flames. Satisfied, he grabbed the can, ducked out the door, pushing it shut.

Already, the windows were glowing.

~ CHAPTER FOUR ~

Each night, Father Frank spent at least forty-five minutes reading from the Bible. Though he had worked late tonight on plans for the fall program of instruction for elementary students, he still kept to his habit of Bible reading. The clock in the living room chimed midnight. As always, he felt refreshed and peaceful after his time with the Bible.

He had just started for his bedroom when he heard the sirens, and they sounded close. He walked onto the front porch. Directly in front of him, not more than a few blocks away, he could see flames leaping into the night sky. He reached back and closed the door and headed for his car.

It took barely two minutes. Four blocks away, Father Frank saw the yellow trucks and the fire fighters working to control the flames. His pulse rate jumped and his throat went dry. He dreaded to see any fire in the community. Now, an added pressure gripped his heart. To his horror, a raging inferno was consuming Calvert Road Baptist Church.

A dozen people stood at a distance watching the spectacle, while others arrived by car and on foot.

Father Frank turned off his car and surveyed the scene. Three police cars fractured the darkness with red, white, and blue strobe lights. Blue bubbles on other vehicles signified volunteers had joined the small group of professional firefighters Pine Tree supported.

The men moved quickly, grim expressions on their faces, focused on trying to minimize the disaster. Orders were shouted out and obeyed with quiet efficiency.

The fire was winning.

The flames lit the area, spotlighting a black Trans-Am with dark tinted windows lurking at the edge of the parking lot. Maybe now was a good time to find out why the driver was hanging around Pine Tree. And the teenagers. And a burning church. The priest started toward the car.

"Can I help you, Father?"

Father Frank cut his eyes right to see a man coming toward him. About six feet tall with broad shoulders, and dark, wavy hair, he wore plain clothes, but his manner and carriage said policeman.

"I'm just going over there to talk to someone," the priest said.

"We'd really like to keep the crowd to a minimum. And we're restricting the movement of civilians around the fire. You need to stay back."

"But ..." Father Frank started to object, then stopped.

It was too late anyway. The car with the tinted windows backed up, cut its wheels and drove away. There would be no confrontation tonight. He looked back at the policeman.

"I'm Father Frank from Prince of Peace. I don't believe I know you."

"Probably not," the policeman answered, but his attention was focused on the fire.

When he said nothing else, Father Frank decided to be more direct.

"And what is your name?"

"Detective Mike Oakley."

"How long have you been on the police force here?"

"Nine years."

"Are you from here?" the priest continued to pry.

"No. Hickory Ridge."

Father Frank opened his mouth to ask another question, but at that moment, a uniformed policeman approached. In the poor light, Father Frank could only make out the last name. Turner.

"Need you over here, Mike."

Mike Oakley abruptly turned and left without a word.

Father Frank continued to watch the flames consume the church. He tried to think of the flames as the power of God, doing something only He could understand. But instead, they looked like the fires of hell, trying to dissuade people from God, destroying a temple erected to give praise to the Lord.

The priest's breathing accelerated. He felt he could see the devil in the flames, lashing out at God, thrashing the people who worshiped in this house of the Lord.

The church served as a gathering place for people to publicly show their devotion to the Almighty. It brought people together for Christian fellowship. The church shone like a beacon, inviting people to come and share in the love of God.

Now the beacon was being reduced to a pile of cinders.

Back at the rectory, Father Frank stood under a hot shower for much longer than normal, scrubbing relentlessly, trying to wash the smell of the smoke from his body, out of his hair. But the acrid scent resided in his brain, along with the image of the church steeple, like praying hands, being consumed by flames.

After Wednesday morning Mass, Father Frank drove to the Calvert Road Baptist Church, or what was left of it. The sight reignited his anger and he struggled to suppress the feeling.

The building burned. The church is the people, their spirit. The church did not burn, only a building where the church met.

A building could be rebuilt. But could the spirit survive such a blow to its body?

Reverend Jack Lee stood perfectly still, hands clasped behind his back, staring at what had been his church. In his mid-forties, he could pass for sixty today. His body sagged and his eyes looked like the grey, lifeless ashes that were the remains of his church building.

Just five years ago, he had taken a small group of parishioners who met in an old house, and convinced them they could build a larger, permanent church, one they could be proud of, and invite others to join. Reverend Lee's prediction had come true. The congregation had doubled in number. Now, the task of building would have to be repeated.

A man in plain clothes, with a clipboard in his hand, was talking with the fire chief. Occasionally, the man picked up a charred piece of debris and examined it. Twice Father Frank watched him put items in a plastic bag and hand them to the fire chief, who wrote several words on labels which he affixed to the bags.

A policeman with *Longview* on his shoulder patch worked with a chocolate Labrador retriever. Father Frank had no idea what the dog was doing but it appeared to be searching for something.

Tendrils of smoke drifted up from a dozen places among the cinders. All that remained of the walls was a small portion of the back wall where the baptistery stood. A mass of charred, still smoldering pages was all that was left of the hymnals. The roof had been reduced to a single, long piece of steel that had been the ridge beam.

Even now, eight or nine hours after the last flame had been extinguished, Father Frank could feel the heat radiating from the fire scene. A slight sulfur odor drifted on the air, making the priest once again think of the devil. Surely his hand was at work in these fires.

Father Frank shook his head. *The fire investigator and the Fire Chief are trying to determine if this was arson. I know the answer. But I can't tell them.* Father Frank pursed his lips and kicked a small rock on the ground. *They'll figure it out. They wouldn't take my word for it anyway, particularly when I couldn't tell them how I know.*

The rock rolled over and stopped in front of Reverend Lee. He turned his head and looked at Father Frank.

"Oh, hello Frank. I didn't hear you drive up. Quite a mess."

Father Frank walked over and put his hand on Reverend Lee's arm. "Jack, I'm so sorry about this. I know how much of your life's blood was in this building."

"I loved this church. Maybe God decided I didn't deserve it." Even as he said it, his eyes became moist.

"This fire wasn't God's doing, Jack. I firmly believe they will determine it was set by man."

The Baptist minister nodded. "Oh, I'm just feeling sorry for myself. It's just... such a waste. All the work we put into this. All the time..." He looked down at the ground and shook his head.

"You have a strong congregation. They'll rebuild."

Reverend Lee looked up and tried to smile. "You're right. They're a good bunch and we will rebuild, but it will take so many resources that could have been directed to other worthy projects. I feel like we've stolen from those other ministries." His jaw clenched.

"I just get angry when I think of the waste. For what? For nothing. We were beginning to be in a position to help others. Now..." He swept his hand in the direction of the rubble.

Father Frank nodded. "I know what you mean. There's never enough resources, and now, even less. And for no good reason."

He looked around the property. When the Pine Valley Baptist Church burned last week, its education building survived. Though crowded, they were able to hold services on Sunday. Calvert Road Baptist had no other buildings. He laid his hand lightly on Reverend Lee's shoulder.

"If Prince of Peace can help at all, please call me. Our church is available between ten-thirty and four-thirty Sundays, if you want to use it. I know it's not the same. But if you need a place, we'd like to help."

Once again, tears threatened to escape Reverend Lee's eyes. For a moment he said nothing, and when he did speak, his voice trembled.

"That is most generous. Thank you. I've got several of our deacons working on housing. If they don't come up with something by tomorrow, I may take you up on that offer."

During the drive back to Prince of Peace guilt draped over Father Frank, dragging his spirit down.

Somehow, he felt responsible, as if he could have prevented this fire. But he didn't know there was going to be another fire. Certainly, he did not know another church would be targeted. What could he have done? Turned the police on Sammie? Let them try to sweat out of him what he knew?

Father Frank honestly believed that Sammie did not know about this fire in advance. *Why do you think that?* He shook his head, not knowing the answer.

Sammie hadn't mentioned another fire. He sounded genuinely distraught about his part in the first fire. Surely he would have mentioned plans for another fire, if he had known.

Maybe Sammie knew nothing about this second fire until his parents were talking about it over breakfast, or one of his friends told him? Father Frank shook his head again. Or when the arsonist drove to the site and set the blaze.

Sammie is basically a good kid. He may be traveling with the wrong people right now, but Sammie wouldn't be an active part in burning a church. He was at Mass last Sunday. He'll be at Mass next Sunday. How could he burn a church of God?

He thought about Sammie and his unwillingness to tell what he knew. Was that some sort of loyalty? Some teenage code of conduct? You don't squeal on your friends? But do you need a friend who would commit such an act?

Father Frank decided that had to fit into a sermon in the near future. A person must make decisions based on what is right, not on what a friend wants. That needed a little refining but the basic idea of decision making was spot-on. Why wait? Now was the time. Give the sermon next Sunday. Maybe it would put a little pressure on Sammie to tell the police what he knows.

The temperature continued to climb. The sun hovered overhead with not a single wisp of a cloud to impede its radiant heat. A drop of sweat ran down Father Frank's neck and under his collar. He regretted not leaving his Roman collar in the car. In his haste to get to the basketball game, he had forgotten how hot it was today.

The Bisons were playing the Bobcats in the third game of the morning and the boys were running around the basketball court unaware, or at least unimpressed, that the thermometer had long since passed the ninety degree mark.

Ah, the advantages of youth, Father Frank thought.

He had tried to get the school district to open up the high school gym for his summer league. After all, it was not a church function but an activity for all the teenage boys of Pine Tree during the summer when there was little to occupy their time. The superintendent had refused.

First, it was the custodial problem and the cleaning. When Father Frank offered solutions to those problems, the obstacle became the insurance company. They would not approve it, would cancel the school's policy if the school board allowed this *non-school sponsored* activity. Father Frank suggested that it become a *school sponsored* activity, and that he would do all the organizing, overseeing, coordinating, and whatever else.

The school district would need to provide no personnel resources. In fact, they would get a summer program and the credit for a community service, all for the price of opening up the gym. Still the answer was an unwavering *No*. Father Frank didn't believe the school board members were against the summer program, they simply found it easier to not be involved.

Eventually, Father Frank decided it was probably better this way. The games were played out in the open for all to see, and lots of kids dropped by to watch. Some of those had even formed a team and joined for the second round, just because they had seen other kids having fun. Maybe God decided the program worked for more boys when it was outdoors.

While he had managed to get an adult committed to oversee each game, Father Frank came to as many as he could. He believed his presence helped things go smoothly, and he wanted the boys to know he supported them, not just on paper, but with himself.

Besides, he enjoyed watching the young kids having fun playing sports. Many a day, he wondered if he could join an adult league in Tyler as just plain Frank DeLuca, ex-college basketball player who loved the game, and shoot hoops with the best of them. He remembered trying to impress on the UT/Arlington center the importance of a consistent motion in shooting free throws.

"I'll bet I can make five out of ten with my eyes closed," Frank had said.

"No way," the tall, lanky player said.

"Okay. If I can't, I stay and shoot a hundred free throws. But if I make five or more, you shoot a hundred before you quit today."

"Deal."

Frank made seven of the ten, eyes closed. The six foot ten center practiced late that day, eyes open. And his free throw percentage got better.

The Bobcats, aptly named as all three were on the small side, ran circles around the taller Bisons.

Speed is a great weapon, Father Frank thought.

Out of the corner of his eye, he caught a glimpse of a black Trans-Am rounding the corner and creeping along the street next to the basketball court.

The tinted windows made it impossible to see anything about the driver.

But Father Frank felt in his bones the man was studying the boys, looking for his next victim. It was common knowledge that drug dealers operated in Pine Tree. Just the thought of this predator enslaving one of these youngsters to drugs sent the priest's blood pressure soaring.

On impulse, he jumped up and raced to the street. Father Frank stepped in front of the Trans-Am just as the low-slung car started to pick up speed. He put both hands up and stood stock still in its path. Sweat ran down his side. His heart pounded.

~ CHAPTER FIVE ~

On the basketball court, the ball was passed to the skinny kid with a receding chin. The rubber ball flew right on by, banging against the fence. The boy who had thrown the pass began to yell but the skinny kid ignored the shouting. With mouth open but no words coming out, he stretched out his arm, pointing to the street. All eyes turned, focusing on the scene. Father Frank stood in the path of a speeding westbound car, while a delivery truck filled the eastbound lane.

The driver of the Trans-Am slammed on his brakes, all four wheels screaming as they engraved black skid marks on the hot pavement. With nose down, the heavy car skidded to a stop, its front bumper only a foot from Father Frank.

Immediately, the priest raced around and pounded his fist on the driver's window. The car started forward, and Father Frank moved with it, hitting the window again.

The car stopped with a jolt, rocking slightly on its springs. The electric-powered window slid down. Father Frank guessed the driver was in his forties. He had short, dirty-brown hair, a prominent scar across one cheek, a two-day growth of black stubble, and eyes that looked at a person as if measuring him for a coffin. His lantern jaw was locked so tightly, a muscle in his face twitched. When he spoke, it was with a gravel voice that brooked no dissent.

"Get in front of my car again, I'll run over you and never look back." His eyes bored into the priest.

In the bat of an eye, Father Frank's left hand darted into the car and caught the front of the man's shirt. He jerked the man toward the window and spoke softly, his face only inches from the driver.

"If you bring drugs to my kids, I'll personally run over *you*. And I *will* look back. I'll drag you down to the police station."

For tense moments that seemed to drag by in slow motion, the two men glared at each other, neither breaking eye contact, neither blinking. Then, Father Frank let go of the driver's shirt and moved back a step.

The man's expression never changed. He jammed his foot on the accelerator, leaving another long streak of rubber on the hot summer pavement as he sped away.

"Good job last night," Georgia said to Phyllis over the telephone. "I think the POPsters are going to be great."

"It did go well, didn't it?" Phyllis bubbled. "I was so excited, I could hardly sleep."

"I didn't know Roger had a musical background," Georgia said, hoping to pry out more information.

"Yeah. He sang in a choir and a quartet in college. Really liked it. But since he graduated, I don't think he's sung anything except *Happy Birthday*. I'd forgotten how much he enjoyed it. I think he had, too."

"Smart of you to get him involved. So when did you decide to make him the musical director?"

For a moment, Phyllis said nothing. "I don't know. I hadn't thought about it." She paused for a moment. "I don't know much about music. I just volunteered when nobody else did. If he could direct, I could handle the other details."

"Very smart idea. Well, let me know if I can help."

"I think he liked it. Or is that just my wish? You were there last night. What do you think?"

Georgia nodded and smiled, even though Phyllis was five miles away. "My take is he really enjoyed it. And the way he worked with the kids, particularly the boys. He got them to try things I honestly didn't think they would. He's good at it."

"Still, I'm asking him to take on my job."

Georgia hesitated a moment, trying to decide if she might give away her methodology. "Just let him think it's his idea. He sort of took over last night. You could see that he wanted to direct. So, you're willing to let him."

"I'll try that tonight." There was a quick intake of breath. "What if that doesn't work? What do I do then?"

Georgia laughed. "Then, you ask him, sweetly, to do it for you. You feel overwhelmed with everything. It would save your sanity if he would do that for you. And give him a big, passionate kiss."

Phyllis giggled. "I can do that."

Father Frank made a breakfast of scrambled eggs, toast and orange juice. Attendance at today's Mass had been a little better than usual. Maybe it was because of the second church burning in less than a week. Disasters tended to remind people of the God they often forgot. Maybe it reminded them of the fragility of life, the uncertainty, the need to be ready to meet their Maker at any moment. Whatever, he was pleased to see a few more faces at the weekday Mass.

Wouldn't it be nice if so many attended that he wouldn't notice a few extra?

An image of the man in the Trans-Am popped into Father Frank's mind. He felt certain the man was connected to the drug scene in some fashion. The priest had not expected drugs to be a problem in a small, east Texas town. In the last few weeks, he had come to the realization that drugs invaded every place now. Even Pine Tree.

One of the ministers in town told him of a report the police had on the drug problem. It hadn't been made public but the minister knew one of the authors of the report. Father Frank couldn't believe the numbers.

He bristled at the injustice. Before kids were old enough to understand the dangers, they were introduced to the highs, then enslaved by the addiction. How unfair. The kids were not to blame.

Those vipers whose only interest was in making a buck, no matter what the cost to others, were the real villains. They had to bear the full judgment for the evil they sold.

An image of Rick materialized in his mind. He had been Frank's closest friend in high school. Although they went to different schools, they lived only a block apart. And while Frank was a star basketball player, Rick was a top notch baseball player with such a keen eye he never swung at a bad pitch, and seldom struck out.

They liked the same music, many of the same movies, and played long tennis matches during the warm summer months in Dallas. If a Cowboys, Mavericks, or Stars game was on TV, chances were good that Frank and Rick were watching it together. When Frank needed a friend to do something with, or just to talk, Rick was there.

They went to different colleges and their frequent talks ceased. At the Christmas break, Frank learned that Rick had gotten into the drug scene. By midterm, Rick lost his scholarship and dropped out of class. Frank tried to talk to him over the holidays but Rick was never available. A month later, Rick was dead.

He had been a bright student, a talented athlete and the kind of friend who comes along all too rarely. Before he was twenty, he was dead. The undeniable reason—drugs. Frank was depressed for months, almost dropped out of school himself. His dad convinced him to hang in there, work out his grief, and use it to do some good. Frank stayed in school, and vowed to speak out against drugs at every opportunity.

The telephone rang, interrupting Father Frank's worry and mounting anger.

"Hello, Frank. This is Jack, over at Calvert Road Baptist. Or what used to be Calvert Road Baptist."

"And will be again," said Father Frank.

"You remember the old Grace Presbyterian Church, the one they used before building over on Water Street? I've just been talking with Reverend Wilcock there. They've been trying to sell the old facility but nothing has come through yet. They've agreed to let us rent it until we know what we're doing. It's a little small but I think we can crowd into it.

"And that gives us time to decide what to do—build, if that's what we choose, or whatever. They're being very accommodating, no long-term lease or anything. And the rent is reasonable."

"Great. That's not even far for your congregation to go," said Father Frank, genuinely pleased. "What a blessing."

"Well, I wanted to tell you, and also say how much I appreciate your offer. Perhaps we can work together on some ecumenical service or community project. It might be good for both congregations."

"Good idea. We would be open to that. Give me a call when you get settled in your new home. And my offer for Prince of Peace to help still stands."

It was after eleven by the time Father Frank got free and could go see how the basketball league was doing. He turned into the parking lot at City Park, swung the Taurus into one of the two shady spots, shut off the motor and hopped out. He turned toward the basketball court and instantly his pulse rate shot up. Involuntarily, his fists clenched as he took in the scene before him. Standing on the edge of the court, talking to several of the boys, was the man with the Trans-Am. Father Frank eased into a trot.

He pushed in between the man and the boys. "Go on out on the court and start your game," he said to the boys. "Now."

The boys headed for the court. Father Frank grabbed the man by the shirt and pulled him to the side. "I told you to stay away—."

The man's hands shot up, breaking the hold Father Frank had on his shirt. In one fluid motion, his right hand came around and slammed into Father Frank's jaw. The priest went down, conscious, but stunned.

The boys stared with open mouths. Harry Courtright, the biggest among the boys, took a step in the direction of the man who had decked Father Frank. The man turned and fixed Harry with a cold, menacing glare that stopped the teenager dead in his tracks. The man held Harry with his fierce stare until the boy took a step backward.

The man switched his focus to the priest, still on the ground. A moment later, he strode across the asphalt, got into his car and drove off without ever looking back.

Carlos, one of the basketball players, took his gaze off the priest and looked across the park.

"Police car."

He took off at a full run toward the street, his ponytail swinging from side to side. He intercepted the Pine Tree Police Department car and flagged it down. In less than two minutes, Detective Mike Oakley squatted beside Father Frank.

"Are you okay, Father?"

The priest sat up, rubbing his jaw and working it side to side.

"Yeah. I just didn't see it coming. He's got a punch like a jackhammer."

"Come down to the station and file a complaint. You've got plenty of witnesses, and a good case for assault."

Father Frank thought about that for a moment. Would it get the man off the street? Not likely. He shook his head and stood up.

"No. I grabbed him by the shirt first." He turned to the boys. "What did the man want?"

No one spoke. Two boys half-turned away, others suddenly needed to inspect their shoes, or check out the progress of a bug crawling on the ground. Several just shook their heads. Not one word came from the group.

"Does he have a name?" the detective asked. When no answer came, Mike's voice took on a more authoritative tone. "Come on, now. What's his name? What do you call him?"

"Errr," one of the boys mumbled.

Mike moved into policeman mode. "Say his name again, and make it clear this time."

"Earl."

Several heads bobbed up and down in agreement.

"Earl," said Mike. "Any other name? A last name? A nickname? Anything?"

More shakes of heads. A couple said, "Nah."

A boy with a bad case of acne said, "Earl is the only thing he told us."

Father Frank asked, "What did he want?"

Again, silence.

"Was he trying to sell you drugs?" Father Frank looked at the boy who had flagged down the detective.

"Come on, Carlos. Earl was talking. You have ears. What was he saying?"

Carlos looked like he wanted to shrink into the ground. "He, um, he wanted to know, um, who had drugs. Where he could find some."

"Is that all?"

"He asked if we knew who ran the show here," said Chip, the kid with almost no chin.

Father Frank nodded several times. "And what did you tell him?"

Chip's eyes opened wide and he shook his head. "Nothing. I don't know none of that stuff." He looked at the detective. "I'm not into that stuff. I mean, I know it's around, but I don't know nothing about it."

"We're not accusing you of anything," said Mike. We're just trying to find out what that guy is doing here. That's all."

Carlos spoke up. "Honest, Father, that's all it was. He was asking us what we knew and we all said, 'Nothing.' We don't know anything about that stuff. Except that it's in school. But none of us ever tried it."

He looked at the boys around him. Several of them nodded enthusiastically.

"Good," said Mike, drawing the boys' attention back. "Don't ever start. Some of the new stuff can make you an addict the very first time you try it. Stay away from it." He gave each of the boys a stern look.

Father Frank smiled at them, trying to ease the tension.

"Thanks for the help. Now, go on and finish your warm-up. I don't want to be the cause of you getting behind schedule. I'm okay, and you've told the detective what he needed to know. I want to talk to the detective for a few minutes."

The boys left quickly, happy to be away from the questions, and in a minute or two, they were running and yelling as if nothing had happened.

Father Frank turned to Mike. "Do you know anything about this Earl guy?"

"Nothing. I've seen his black Trans-Am cruising the streets the last few days, maybe a week. He's new on the scene. Never done anything to cause us to stop him, or check him out."

"How about now?"

"I will today. By slugging you, he's gotten on the radar. And with what the kids said about Earl's interest in drugs, we'll have to keep an eye on him. I'll see what D.M.V. has on him, and go from there. He's probably in our database."

A shout went up from the basketball court as Carlos sank a three-point shot. "How was that, Father?" he yelled.

Father Frank nodded his approval and gave the boy a thumbs-up. He turned back to Mike.

"Any news on the church fires?"

"Not much. Got someone out from the State Fire Marshall's office in Tyler. He determined the fires were definitely arson. Of course, after the second church fire in less than a week we'd already decided they were arson. He brought in the accelerant dog out of Longview. Found diesel was used in both fires."

"Accelerant dog?"

"An arson dog."

Father Frank nodded. "I saw an officer with a dog at Calvert Baptist."

"Dog's a big help. He can tell if an accelerant was used. And with his super-sensitive nose, he can spot the point of origin," Mike said. "Saves a lot of work and time for the officers."

The men stood in silence for a minute, grim expressions on their faces.

"I'm more than a little interested in both the church fires. And Earl," said Father Frank. "I really don't like to see him talking with my kids. You will let me know what you find out?"

"Sure." The detective shifted his feet and assumed a more relaxed position. "And you have to tell me what happened with you. I was at UT Arlington when you played there. Then, after your sophomore year you left. You had an opportunity to be a star. Already were on our campus."

Father Frank laughed. "And nobody knew me five miles away."

"Not true. I remember watching you make an incredible steal—quickest hands I've ever seen—then race down the floor and sink a three-point shot at the buzzer to beat SMU. Absolutely amazing. The Mustangs had a two point lead *and* the ball with four seconds to go, and you beat them. I couldn't believe it. Neither could SMU."

"Just luck."

But the priest couldn't keep a tiny smile from creeping onto his face, pleased—and amazed—that someone remembered what was undoubtedly his best play in two years of college basketball.

"I said that was the most incredible play I'd ever seen and what a great player you were. This absolute drop-dead beauty sitting in the seat in front of me turned and said she dated you."

The image of Ginger Hamilton materialized in Father Frank's mind—a long-legged, slender, black-haired beauty whose eyes always seemed to be excited over some mystery they concealed. Frank had thought of her as simply elegant, a true lady.

Frank and Ginger had been very compatible, at ease with one another, yet with a sexual tension that kept two hearts racing. She had been a strong temptation not to follow his vocation. But God's call overpowered Ginger's.

A few months ago, he heard from a college friend that she had married an engineer last year and moved to Oregon.

Mike turned serious. "You were becoming a star, you had a knockout girl, and you disappeared. What happened?"

Father Frank cocked his head to one side. "I got a better opportunity."

Mike wrinkled his brow and looked at the priest.

Father Frank grinned. "I got the chance to do God's work. As much as I loved basketball, and still do, God's work is a far better opportunity. No question."

~ CHAPTER SIX ~

"**W**hat do you think?" Georgia looked expectantly at Phyllis.

The two women stood in the church hall, waiting for the POPsters to arrive for rehearsal.

"I don't know. That's awfully soon."

"You told me you thought they were doing great. And I agree. Why not reward them for the hard work?"

Again, Georgia's body, with subtle movements of her head and shoulders, urged the unsure woman in front of her. Georgia saw she was losing.

"You and Roger have done amazing things with them in just a few rehearsals. Let them sing at Sunday's Mass and they'll work even harder. And what a nice gift to the Lord—twenty-five young voices singing His praise."

Georgia had reached her limit. The pronouncement had to come from Phyllis. Georgia would make it work, but Phyllis had to make the decision. She had to take charge and lead.

Dear Jesus, please help her see this is the right thing to do.

Phyllis twisted her mouth and wrinkled her forehead. She wiggled her head from left to right.

Fear. Georgia could see that was the problem. Phyllis worried she might make a mistake. For Georgia, decisions offered a chance to shape the future, to help determine how things would happen. She viewed decisions as opportunities, not problems.

Phyllis inhaled deeply. "I'll suggest it to the kids tonight. And Roger, of course. If they're enthusiastic about it, we'll do it." She did not look confident. "Oh, and I'll have to ask Father Frank if it's okay."

"Good idea," said Georgia. "He usually stops by rehearsals." She had already floated the idea by Father Frank, and he was enthusiastic. But she knew he would be discreet when Phyllis asked him.

"What will they sing?"

"Ah, the advantage of having a musical director. Let Roger select the songs. You pick the director, he picks the songs. And you picked a good man."

"Yes, I did. Not only for musical director but also for a husband." A big smile erased all the worry lines that had inhabited her face moments earlier.

Thirty minutes later, most of the kids were milling around the rehearsal room, visiting as if they hadn't seen each other in a month.

When Roger arrived, he joined Phyllis and Georgia. Phyllis wasted no time. "What do you think about having the kids sing at Sunday's Mass?"

For five seconds, Roger pondered the question and Phyllis's face began to sag. "If you don't think—"

"No. No. Great idea. I was just running through songs in my mind, deciding which ones we could sing. Let's ask the kids."

He turned toward the teenagers and snapped his fingers a few times to get their attention. "What say we sing at next Sunday's Mass?"

A moment of silence was followed by a cacophony of responses ranging from, "No way we're ready," to "Yeah" and "Cool."

In the end, Hillary Lindale, already a beauty at fifteen, quieted the others and said, "If you think we're ready for it, Mister Traynor, then I say let's go for it. Right, guys?"

"I think you're ready," said Roger.

"Let's do it," came the response.

Midway through the practice, Father Frank wandered into the hall. Worry lines began to appear on Phyllis' face. She glanced at Georgia, took a deep breath, and headed over to talk to the priest. She fidgeted and could hardly meet his eyes, but in only a minute, she smiled, her shoulders straightened and she turned to deliver a positive nod to Georgia.

From behind Phyllis, Father Frank winked at Georgia.

At the end of the next song, Phyllis approached the chorus. "Good news, guys. Father Frank said he would be delighted to have you sing at Sunday's Mass."

Cheers and whoops poured out from the teenagers amid high-fives and slaps on the back.

"Okay, guys," said Roger. "We've got lots of work to do to be ready. But, let's take a ten minute break. Then I'll lay out the program for you—what songs we'll sing and when. Ten minutes. Not eleven."

The group broke up, many headed for the restrooms, some for bottles of water, and some just to visit with friends. Ethan, a short, handsome boy who played on the Bobcats team in Father Frank's summer basketball league approached the priest.

"Er, Father. Got a minute?"

"Sure. What's on your mind?"

Ethan fidgeted with his shirt tail, looked around, and down at the floor. The priest realized this was not a comfortable place for Ethan to bring up whatever it was he wanted to talk about.

"Why don't we walk outside, where it's not so noisy?"

Ethan nodded, relief flooding his features.

Father Frank led the way out the back door to a small patio with several benches and a few potted plants. The sun appeared to be balanced on one of the pine trees that lined the church property. A gentle breeze kept the temperature pleasant. No sign of rain today. The priest looked around and found no one else in sight.

"How's this?"

Ethan still looked uncomfortable, but nodded.

"Is something bothering you, Son?" Father Frank asked.

"Sort of. You've been asking about that Earl guy, and drugs and things."

"Yes," the priest prompted.

"Well, there's a guy who dropped out of school this year. B.D. I don't know what that stands for, but that's what everybody calls him. Well, he's gotten into drugs. I don't know much else about him but I know he's into them. I think that's why he dropped out."

"You know his last name? Where he lives?"

"No. Just B.D. is all."

"What's he look like?"

"He's about your height and has red hair. Oh, and a tattoo of a dragon on his arm. Right arm, I think. Rides a blue motorbike. He hangs out at The Corral a lot. At least that's what he says. That's a pool hall out on Road 2140, just outside the city limits."

When Ethan said nothing else, Father Frank said, "I'll check on him. Anything else on your mind?"

"No. "

"You didn't tell me that when I asked all you guys the other day." He avoided any note of disapproval in his tone.

Ethan looked down at his shoes, and kicked an imaginary rock, then rubbed his right leg with his left shoe.

"Um, I didn't want to sound like a snitch or something. Nobody else said anything."

"I'm glad you told me today. And remember, Ethan, telling what you know to help solve a crime, or maybe save someone from getting into even worse trouble, is not a bad thing. In fact, if you can help someone by telling what you know, that's a good thing. Nothing to be ashamed of."

Father Frank put his hand on the boy's shoulder. "It was definitely the right thing to do. I won't mention this to any of the other guys. Thanks for telling me."

Ethan looked relieved but said nothing.

"You don't go out to The Corral, do you?" Father Frank asked casually, no accusation in his voice.

Ethan's eyes opened wide. "The Corral? No. Not me. I wouldn't go out there on a bet."

"Good. I don't think it's a place for... actually, not a good place for anybody."

But, I'm going out there.

~ CHAPTER SEVEN ~

After Friday morning Mass, Father Frank worked in his office, answering a questionnaire from the diocese, returning two phone calls, paying several parish bills, and updating some parish records in the computer. He finished sending an e-mail to the woman in charge of the Prince of Peace bulletin and glanced at his watch. If he hurried, he could catch the last few minutes of today's basketball games.

He whipped into the parking lot, and breathed a little easier when he saw no sign of Earl or the black Trans-Am. The boys were running, yelling, and having a good time expending some of their boundless energy in a wholesome activity.

Several of the boys watching the game threw up a hand to wave at Father Frank. The priest waved back, a big smile on his face.

This is the way a teenager's summer should be. Running, playing, enjoying their youth.

By 11:40, Father Frank was driving east, heading out to The Corral. Shortly after arriving in Pine Tree, he had heard about the bar, its location, and reputation as the center for heavy drinking. More recently, he'd heard it called a cog in local drug movement.

About half a mile outside the town limits, a notch was cut into the thick pine groves that lined the highway. The priest turned into a large parking lot that had once been graveled.

Parked in haphazard fashion was a mixture of motor-cycles, a mud-covered pickup, two or three souped-up cars, and a number of junkers. A lone bicycle leaned against a tree that showed the scars of several mishaps. Bottles and cans littered the area, as well as bits of newspapers, empty chip bags, candy wrappers, and empty packaging from cigarettes and a variety of other items. A tennis shoe dangled from a lower branch of a pine tree at the edge of the parking area.

The building itself was even less impressive. It had been constructed probably fifty years ago as a café at the edge of town on the road leading to Smithboro. Now, a much better highway existed only a mile to the east, capturing most of the traffic between the two towns.

Father Frank doubted the structure had been painted since it was built. The roof had a definite sway to it, emulating a tired old horse penned in The Corral. What had once been front windows were now boarded up with scrap lumber. In amongst the graffiti that decorated the building, Father Frank could make out the hours of operation: 11 am to 2 am.

It also claimed they served hot dogs and hamburgers in addition to beer and liquor. From what he had heard, the drinks outnumbered the food five hundred to one. Although it was not his habit to do so in Pine Tree, he locked the car when he got out.

The door opened to a room so filled with smoke Father Frank could not make out much more than two pool tables in the middle and a bar on the left. The clack of pool balls mixed with raucous laughter and loud voices.

Slowly, his eyes adjusted to the darker interior. He thought he had been in some seedy places when he was a freshman in college, but nothing came close to this.

The men inside—Father Frank saw no women as he scanned the room—matched the vehicles outside. Some projected the stereotypical look of bikers. Two others looked like good candidates for owners of the souped-up vehicles. A huge man in dirty overalls probably drove the mud-caked truck.

Behind the bar, a large man wearing a muscle shirt that exposed tattoos from wrists to shoulders eyed him suspiciously. Father Frank regretted not removing his Roman collar but it was too late now. He walked to the bar, trying to assess the men around the room.

"What'll it be?" the bartender barked.

"A Coke, please."

"You came in here for a Coke? Does this look like a Coke kind of place?"

Father Frank grinned and tried to look as pleasant and friendly as possible.

"Actually, I was looking for a person. Goes by the initials B.D. He wouldn't happen to be here, would he?"

The barman leaned his head back and guffawed. "He wouldn't happen to be. He ain't."

"Do you expect him in today?"

"Buddy, I learnt not to expect nothing of nobody. You ain't gonna get no information here."

Father Frank nodded several times and moistened his lips with his tongue. "You see him, would you tell him Father Frank from Prince of Peace would like to talk to him?"

"Oh, you can count on it," the big man said. He let out another laugh.

The sweet smell of marijuana invaded the priest's nose. He looked at the odd collection of patrons and decided much harder stuff changed hands and was likely consumed on premises.

Father Frank turned to leave and found himself face to face with Earl. The man's flint-like eyes bored into the priest like hot pokers. The shock of the encounter and the intensity of the man's gaze made it difficult to maintain contact, yet impossible to break away. Father Frank opened his mouth to speak but nothing came out. Earl leaned forward, bringing his face within inches of his quarry.

"Stick to preaching," Earl said, barely above a whisper, but carrying the weight of a shout. "This ain't a game of b-ball." For a long moment, he held the priest's attention.

Abruptly, Earl turned and strode over to one of the patrons and grabbed him by the shirt. Father Frank wondered why the man wore a long sleeved shirt in this hot weather. The sleeves were turned up at the cuffs. Hollow eyes with dilated pupils seemed not to focus on anything.

The man was one of those Father Frank had pegged as a drug user. When Earl grabbed the man's shirt, it pulled his sleeves up higher, revealing what were probably needle tracks along the inside of his forearm.

Earl yanked the man forward, bringing him in close, raising him to his tiptoes. As unaware as the man seemed before, Earl had his full attention now. Father Frank watched for a few moments, saw the man cringe under Earl's ferocity. Whatever Earl was saying to the man appeared to raise his cognizance and instill fear. But from across the room, the priest could hear no words, just a low, modulated rumble. Even so, he could sense the power, the dominance Earl exerted.

Father Frank walked out of the grungy building, happy to breathe fresh air again. The black car with the dark-tinted windows rubbed elbows with his Taurus. He stepped over and cupped his hand against the windshield, trying to cut the glare and look inside the Trans-Am. He could see nothing on the dash or either of the bucket seats. The heavily tinted side windows prevented any view there.

The priest was not certain what to make of his encounter with Earl. Did Earl issue a threat today, like the one he made before? And how seriously should the priest take it?

At least he didn't try to man-handle me like he did the other man.

Just what was Earl's position in the drug scene? Maybe Father Frank needed Earl's address more than B.D.'s. But he could find Earl. Just look around during a basketball game and the Trans-Am would probably be cruising by.

Father Frank looked at this watch. He had to visit three parishioners who were in the hospital and he had just enough time to get there at his usual hour. Mrs. Nutley thought he should arrive precisely at 1:15 and would be either worried or upset if he were late.

Moments later, the Corral disappeared in his rearview mirror.

Hospital rounds provided no bad news or shocks, which made for a good trip. He delivered the sacrament of the Eucharist to two of the patients. With each, he sat and visited, listening to whatever they wanted to talk about. The first was a frail man, who focused on his current problems—how the medication upset his stomach, his problem getting pain pills often enough, the lack of attention the doctor gave him. Father Frank exuded sympathy.

Next, he went to see Mrs. Nutley, a woman in her nineties who might not live to get out of the hospital. She reminisced about her childhood friends, many of whom she had not seen in seventy years. Father Frank listened carefully, asking pertinent questions and displaying interest in each incident from the distant past.

After he left her, he stopped to visit and pray with the parents of a small child who had somehow contracted hepatitis B and, while expected to recover, was not doing well at the moment. Father Frank found it very difficult to console parents who could see no earthly reason why their young, innocent child should suffer. "God's will be done," worked better for an adult than a blameless child.

Just after 3:00, Father Frank again turned into the Corral's parking lot. The number of cars had more than doubled since noon. A few he remembered from the morning: a shiny green Chevy with no hood, the Golden Eagle motorcycle, the van that looked like something from a sixties movie. But no black Trans-Am adorned the littered parking lot. He removed his Roman collar, and again locked his car.

If anything, the smoke was thicker, and the marijuana more pronounced, than during his earlier visit. He could imagine getting high just breathing the air in the building. Another distinct smell which the priest did not recognize mingled with that of the marijuana.

Slowly he checked the patrons. He didn't see a tall redhead with a dragon decorating his arm. This time, Father Frank asked the burly bartender for a beer.

He handed the priest the bottle, and said, "That's better, but I still don't know no B.D., and if I did know him, I ain't seen him."

Father Frank ambled over to one of the pool tables, leaned against the wall and watched a few shots. A short, round man scratched an eight ball, slammed ten dollars down on the table and with a string of curses, left, tossing his cue stick in the direction of the rack.

A man with his left hand missing picked up the bill and stuck it in his pocket. He looked at Father Frank and said, "Sawbuck a game, if you got the guts."

Basketball was Frank's first love in sports. But there had been a pool table in the athletic facility at UTA, and Frank found it very relaxing to shoot a little eight ball before a basketball game. He had become quite good at it.

Father Frank lagged his ball two inches from the rail and won the break. He sank a ball on the break and proceeded to drop two more with rather difficult shots. Father Frank tried to maintain his concentration, but couldn't ignore the attention the game drew. When he sank the next two balls, the noise level in the room dropped noticeably. His next shot was not as difficult but he missed it.

His opponent may have been missing a hand, but that didn't hamper him when it came to handling a pool cue. He rested the cue on the stump of his arm. It seemed unlikely a person could control it very well that way but he had mastered that skill. He had a shot to win the game and missed it by an eighth of an inch, the ball just catching the corner of the pocket, probably because the ball had to travel over a small tear in the felt that had been glued down.

With that opening, Father Frank ran his remaining two stripes and then called the eight ball in the side pocket.

Without a word, the man threw the ten dollars he had won earlier on the table and racked his stick.

"Tell you what," said Father Frank. "I'd rather have B.D.'s address and last name than the ten dollars. And I'll throw in this bottle of beer I haven't touched."

The man looked at him, the ten dollars, and the beer. He grabbed the bottle and drank half of it in one slug, then put it down.

"Name's Rake. Lives in a shack out on the lake road, maybe half mile past the dump turnoff."

He scooped up the ten dollars, stuffed it in his pocket, picked up the bottle and walked away.

As Father Frank turned to go, he heard a snicker and looked over to one of the booths. A beefy man with pea eyes and a golf-ball nose stared at him. He wore a scraggly mustache and tattoos decorated his forearms. The man held something in one hand, and with the other hand, he swiped a match on his dirty pants, lighting it. He held the burning match in front of him for a moment, and held the priest's attention.

Now Father Frank could make out what was clutched in the man's other hand. He had fashioned a cross out of paper napkins. A smirk materialized on the man's face and he moved the flame under the cross. It took only a second for the paper cross to burst into flames. The fire raced up the paper.

Father Frank was mesmerized, the orange flames burning into his retina. Now he was seeing a church burning, a hot, pulsing fire devouring a place of worship, and the cross toppling into the inferno.

The fire reached the man's stubby fingers. He threw the burning paper on the floor and crushed it with his boot. His focus never left the priest. A disturbing laugh shook his considerable belly, and erupted from his mouth. Not a joyful laugh. It was the laugh of the mad scientist concocting some evil potion.

All conversation stopped. Half of the people stared at Father Frank and half at the man who was laughing. The laugh and the sickly smirk revolted the priest, but he couldn't tear his focus from the man. Father Frank had to physically shake his head to tear his gaze away from the man. The priest started for the door, feeling as though he were not controlling his feet, as if the flames had burned his equilibrium.

Even in the car, his mind replayed the scene of the man burning the paper cross. The evil laugh resonated in the priest's brain. And then, it hit him with the force of a punch to the chest. Like the man in The Corral, the arsonist *enjoyed* it. He *enjoyed* burning the churches.

Did he smile when he splashed the diesel around the church? Laugh as he tossed on the match? Father Frank put his head on the steering wheel and tried to purge the image from his mind. He had focused on the tragedy of burning churches and had difficulty dealing with it. The realization that someone actually took pleasure in the act threw the priest into a state of despair.

Several minutes seeped away before he managed to tear his mind from this new horror. He forced his brain to concentrate on other things, anything that did not involve a burning church.

About a mile down the road, he looked up at the cloud-speckled sky.

Lord, I wasn't really gambling. I was buying information. Trying to save a church.

~ CHAPTER EIGHT ~

Father Frank finished Saturday Mass, changed and walked out the front door. Mrs. Zimmerman was waiting for him.

"I hate to be the angel of bad news, but I am."

"Well, it's a beautiful day, the sun is shining, but not too hot, and I've just said Mass. I should be able to take it," said Father Frank, a twinkle in his dark eyes.

The fiftyish woman, tall, thin and not generally given to levity, did not smile back.

"I hope so," she said, as serious as an accountant at tax time.

Father Frank tried to remember if he had ever seen the woman smile. Maybe he could tell her a joke and coax out a tiny bit of a smile. A priest and a rabbi sat in a bar, talking with a white rabbit. No... he seriously doubted it. On the plus side, though, he had never seen Mrs. Zimmerman angry either.

Right now, she looked grim.

"All four of the tires on your Taurus are flat. Looks like someone took a knife to them."

Father Frank's head twisted to the right, and his stomach twisted in a knot. "All four?"

"All four. I walked all the way around the car."

Without another word, he hurried over to the parish car. A cool breeze ruffled the leaves of the redbud tree, and a nuthatch flew in to perch on one of its branches, but Father Frank could see nothing but the tires. He checked all four. Each was as flat as a fifty-cent pancake, with a ragged slash through the sidewall.

His spirit sagged. The Taurus needed new tires, but he didn't want to be forced into replacing them immediately. He drew his lips into a thin, straight line. Cuts in the sidewall of a tire generally could not be repaired. Good time or not, he would have to buy new tires. He couldn't even drive the car, and didn't even know where to get tires. He shook his head as he realized he had never bought tires. He didn't have a car in college. And neither of the two parish cars he'd used since leaving the seminary had needed new tires. Until now.

Mrs. Zimmerman had followed him over to the car. "Dan doesn't have much going on today. I'll have him bring his little truck over for you to use until you can get new tires."

Her husband, recently retired, used a small Ford Ranger pickup to do odd jobs for neighbors.

"That would be terrific." Father Frank forced a smile. "And now you are an angel of good news. Needless to say, I'll be here."

Detective Mike Oakley squatted down studying the driveway. "If you had a dirt driveway, instead of this asphalt, I could probably find some clues. Nothing I can see on this stuff. No foot prints, no tire prints. Nothing."

"I think it's only on TV that the police find all those clues." Father Frank was working hard to be upbeat.

"No. We often find some significant clues at a crime scene. Clues that actually help convict a person in court." He straightened up. "Not today. And in rubber, we can't even get an idea about the knife. We're out of luck."

"It was worth a try."

"You got any idea who might have done this? You made anybody mad lately? Refused to give the sacraments to anybody?"

The priest laughed. "No. You hear about that but it's very rare. I won't withhold the sacraments from anyone. The Lord will decide if a person is worthy or not. My job is to provide help, support, guidance. Not to judge."

He thought about his visit to The Corral yesterday. No reason for anyone there to be angry. And he hadn't found B.D. Rake yet. He shook his head.

"Can't think of anyone."

"How 'bout that guy who decked you the other day? Earl something."

For a moment, the scene with Earl at The Corral and his comment about sticking to preaching popped into the priest's mind. Somehow, Earl did not seem like the tire slashing type. Church burning? Maybe.

He shook his head. "Doesn't seem like his style. And if he did it, he'd do it while I was watching."

"Well, if you think of anyone, give me a call and I'll check 'em out." The detective turned to go, then stopped. "Who's that over there, coming out of that building? The young one."

Father Frank looked over. "That's Georgia Peitz."

"Looks like a peach to me. Married?"

The priest had to smile. It had been a long time since he had wondered whether a woman was married or not. "No."

"Peitz. I knew a Leo Peitz several years ago. Didn't really know him. He was a medical technician and sometimes we were at the same accident scene. He joined up and went to Iraq. Got killed, I don't know, maybe a couple of years ago."

"That was her husband. It was three years ago. She had a rough time for a while, but I think she's come to terms with it now."

She was standing in the shade of an oak tree. The sun had picked its way through the leaves to highlight Georgia's auburn hair, making it look like spun gold. Even from this distance, one could see the sparkle in her eyes. Mike was still staring at her.

"Does she date?"

Father Frank laughed. "I wouldn't know. You'll have to ask her that yourself."

"Okay. Come on. Introduce me."

"Now?"

"What better time? She's here, I'm here." Mike grinned. "And you're indebted to me."

"And how am I indebted to you?"

"You need the police. That's me. I'm going to help you find who slashed your tires. You're going to introduce me to that gorgeous woman. Let's go."

As they approached, Father Frank could hear Georgia's take charge tone, talking with another parishioner.

"We'll lay out the committees you need and an outline of the first couple of meetings. Then, you contact people whom you believe will be good committee chairpersons. We can get the first part done this week. I'll help you. It'll be fun."

The woman offered her thanks and left.

"Georgia," Father Frank began. "This is Mike Oakley, a Detective with the Pine Tree Police Department. Mike, this is Georgia Peitz."

They exchanged pleasantries and then Mike said, "Would you like to go out to dinner with me tonight?"

A tiny smile crossed her face, and Georgia, whom Father Frank had never known to be at a loss for words, said nothing.

Mike pushed forward. "It's got to be okay. Your priest introduced us. He'll vouch for me. So will the police department. And my mother. What kind of restaurants do you like?"

"Ah, well, ah, places with good fresh vegetables," she stammered.

"How does seven-thirty sound? Or would you prefer six-thirty? Your choice."

Father Frank had managed to keep from laughing out loud. But he decided he couldn't restrain himself much longer. "I think I'll run along."

Georgia's eyebrows shot up. "No. Don't leave yet, Father."

"I won't bite," said Mike, looking amused.

Georgia was clearly flustered. "No, no. I didn't mean that. I mean, I need to talk with Father Frank about some parish business."

"Fine," said Mike. "Six-thirty or seven-thirty?"

"Seven-thirty."

"I'll pick you up at seven-thirty. Until then."

Mike turned and strode off, with a spring in his step Father Frank had not noticed earlier. He and Georgia watched the young officer cross to his car, get in and drive off.

"What did I just do?" Georgia asked, her emerald eyes open wide.

"I'd say you just accepted a date."

"I guess I did." She tilted her head to one side. "I haven't done that in a long, long time. Since maybe two years before Leo and I married."

"Maybe it's time you did. And Mike seems like a nice person. But then, I don't really know much about him. And I am *not* endorsing him, contrary to what he said. You're on your own there."

"Thanks a lot." She frowned and looked at the priest. "He didn't ask me where I live."

"He *is* a detective, Georgia. If he can't find you, I'll be disappointed in him."

"What a day. I've just agreed to help organize a Prince of Peace Ladies' Guild, we've got a final practice before the POP-sters' first public performance, and now I think I just accepted a date, ah, an invitation for dinner."

"There's no 'think' about it. You accepted. A policeman will be coming to pick you up. Maybe in a squad car, with lights flashing. Maybe the siren blaring. Who knows?" The priest grinned. "And the proper word *is* 'date', Georgia. Not 'invitation.' You're going on a date."

A horn honked, and both turned to see Dan Zimmerman in his Ranger, sitting behind the Taurus with its four flat tires.

"There's my ride for the day. Got to run. Good luck tonight," Father Frank said.

"If you'll drive me home," said Dan, "you can have the truck until Monday afternoon." He got in the passenger side.

Father Frank slid behind the wheel, adjusted the seat back a little farther from the steering wheel and started the truck.

"I hope I won't need it that long. But thanks. I have a number of visits I need to make today, plus I've got to make arrangements to get somebody over here and put on four tires."

"Got anybody in mind?"

"No. I'm open to suggestions."

"Well, Vic Lindale—he's a member of the parish—has a tire shop on Main, next to the carwash. I used him a couple of months ago and was pleased with his work and prices. I'd try him first. If he can't get to it, there's a place on two forty-four that can probably take care of you."

"Thanks. This is a big help."

"No problem. Turn left at the next corner," Dan pointed. "Our house is the second one on the right. I told Roger I'd help him move some stuff Monday after he got off work. I don't need the truck until then."

Father Frank pulled to stop in front of a neat, white frame house with a lush garden of flowers all across the front. Dan opened the door to get out.

"Just don't get four flats on my truck."

~ Chapter Nine ~

Father Frank checked his watch. Eleven twenty Saturday morning might not be the best time to find B.D. at home, but Father Frank aimed the truck toward the lake road.

He had hoped to make this trip earlier, but priestly duties took longer than he planned. He had delivered the Sacrament of Eucharist to two shut-in parishioners, and naturally each wanted to talk. He enjoyed visiting with the elderly, listening to stories from a time before he was born. Today, he wanted to find a clue to the church burnings.

The third person he visited was an invalid woman with only one family member in the area, a niece who worked long hours. The old woman's vision was almost gone, so reading was out of the question and even television was difficult. In the year he had known her, he had never heard her complain.

When he arrived, she had a radio on but it appeared to be more for noise than entertainment. The woman asked him to say the rosary with her and of course he could not refuse.

He let the truck roll to a stop opposite a dented mailbox balanced on top of a wooden post that wobbled in the breeze. An address but no name was scrawled on one side. Father Frank looked up and down the road and saw no other houses. He felt confident he had found the right place.

B.D.'s unpainted house couldn't have been much larger than a double car garage. Two weathered planks sitting on some bricks served as the front porch. Pieces of plywood covered one of the two small windows in the front. Old newspapers were taped on the inside of the other window. A faded blue motorbike lay on its side in the dirt by the porch.

At least it doesn't have flat tires, Father Frank thought.

He sat there for a minute, doubt making him hesitate. Was he meddling in something that was none of his business? An image of a burning church flashed across his mind. It was his business.

Other than the motorbike, there was no sign of anyone being there: no lights, no music, no noise at all. Just the wind soughing in the trees. Still, a prickling at the back of his neck gave him the distinct feeling he was being watched.

He knocked on the door. No response. He rapped a little harder.

When no one answered, he banged hard on the door and called out, "B.D., this is Father Frank from Prince of Peace Church. I'd like to talk to you for a couple of minutes."

"He ain't here," a wary voice from within answered.

"Then, let me talk to you for a minute."

"No. Go away. He ain't here."

Father Frank tilted his head to one side and thought about it. The motorbike convinced him B.D. was in there. He knocked again.

"I'm not going away."

As he stopped knocking, he heard a door open, the rusty hinges squeaking. And then, the soft slap of sneakers on dirt. Father Frank jumped off the porch and looked around the side of the house. Racing away from him was a skinny kid, a mop of copper-colored hair flying in the breeze.

Father Frank would have bet a tattoo decorated the young man's right arm.

The kid had a good head start on Father Frank, but speed had been one of the priest's strong points. He had always believed he could outrun anyone on the basketball court. Taking off after B.D., the priest caught him within a hundred yards. Father Frank grabbed his arm and pulled him to a stop.

"I just want to talk with you, that's all."

The tattooed dragon guided B.D.'s hand into his pocket and pulled out a switchblade knife. With a quick flick, he flipped open a six-inch blade.

"Go away and leave me alone."

Father Frank didn't feel in danger. While the knife looked deadly enough, B.D. did not. The boy's bloodshot eyes jerked from side to side but didn't seem to focus on anything. He rocked slightly, as if having trouble keeping his balance.

The priest spoke softly and slowly. "I'll stay over here. I just want to ask you a few questions."

"I didn't slash your tires. Now, git."

"How'd you know about the tires?"

"Word's out on the street."

"Okay. But I'm not here about tires. I want to know about fires. Do you know anything about the church fires?"

The dragon darted out, taking a swipe at the priest. Father Frank jumped back. His foot hit a fallen tree, and he tumbled to the ground. His quick reflexes had him back on his feet before B.D. could take advantage.

Now emboldened, the boy started to advance, slashing back and forth with the knife. The sun flashed off the blade. The hinges on the house might have been rusty, but B.D. kept the knife well oiled.

Father Frank took another step backward which seemed to encourage B.D., perhaps sensing weakness in his adversary. His eyes glistened and a tiny smirk twisted his mouth. He weighed the knife in his hand. Father Frank could see B.D.'s confidence rising as he crept forward. The priest stopped. B.D. took another step closer, continuing to hack with the switchblade.

The red haired boy was now close enough to make contact. A sneer flickered on his face as his tattooed arm stabbed forward. Father Frank's hand darted out and grabbed the dragon, lifting, twisting, and pulling until the arm was behind B.D.'s back and the knife dropped to the ground.

"Ow! You're hurting me."

"Good. You were trying to hurt me worse."

"Didn't do your tires," B.D. growled. "If I done 'em, that baby truck of yours would still be sittin' on the ground."

Father Frank kicked the knife away and eased the pressure on B.D.'s arm. "What about the church fires? What do you know about them?"

"Nothin'. I don't know nothin' about 'em. Now let go of my arm 'fore I hurt you."

"Who set the fires?"

For an instant, Father Frank saw fear in B.D.'s eyes. Not the pain of a sore arm. Fear. But fear of what? Or whom?

"Come on, B.D. Who's mixed up in the fires? Did you set them?"

"I ain't got nothin' to say to you."

"If you didn't set them, who did?"

"I ain't talkin'." Then quickly, he said, "I don't know nothin' about no fires."

"Come on, B.D. You know who did. Tell me before I twist your arm right off at the shoulder." He gave a little push.

B.D. winced, a small grunt escaping his tightly closed lips. "I don't know nothin' and I ain't sayin' nothin'."

Again, Father Frank saw the fear come into the boy's face. He was six feet tall and eighteen years old, but he was a boy. And he was afraid.

"B.D., tell me who set the fires. I can get the police to protect you. No one will hurt you."

"I don't know nothin'."

"Or I can turn you over to the police and let them charge you on drug use. I'm sure they can find plenty of drugs in your house. Who set the fires?"

This time, B.D. only shook his head. The fear had now established permanent residency.

~ Chapter Ten ~

Father Frank drove back into town and made his way to Lindale Tires. He got out of the truck and went inside. A young man, barely in his twenties approached the priest.

"Can I help you?"

A short, round man with his sleeves rolled up, exposing muscular forearms, looked up from some papers he was reading.

"I'll take this one, Carl." He put the papers under the counter and approached Father Frank, hand outstretched. "Hi, Father. I'm Vic Lindale. We moved here about four months ago. My wife and I, and our daughter, attend Prince of Peace."

"Yes, I've seen you at Mass." Father Frank shook the owner's hand. "Actually, I'm pretty new here myself. I took over the parish just about a year ago."

"What can I do for you today?"

"I need four tires."

Lindale looked past the priest and started out the door. "Well, let's have a look. From here, they don't look that bad."

"No, no. That's not my truck. I have a 2000 Taurus. And right now, all four tires are flat."

The man looked puzzled. "This is a car you drive all the time? And you have *four* flats?"

"Someone cut the sidewalls. I don't think you can repair them. Besides, I needed new tires anyway. Those were hardly worth slashing."

A frown descended over Lindale's face. "Someone slashed all four tires?" He shook his head. "That's just downright mean. Have you called the police?"

"I did, but they didn't find anything. Can you come over to the rectory and put the tires on there?"

"The car's sitting in your drive?"

"Yes."

Lindale worked his lips as if massaging his teeth. "I think the best thing to do is come over, take off all four wheels, bring them back to the shop and mount the new tires here. That way, we can get them balanced properly. Then we'll bring them back over and put the wheels on the car."

"Is it possible to get that done this afternoon?"

Lindale tilted his head and cut his eyes up to look at the ceiling. Father Frank watched the man work his lips as he considered the problem.

"We've got two jobs in the shop right now and another waiting. But I think I can get somebody over there in an hour or so."

He turned to the young man who had first approached Father Frank. "Carl, can you stay on an extra hour today?"

The man nodded.

"If we don't run into any snags, we should be able to have you mobile again by four, four-thirty."

As Father Frank walked back to Zimmerman's truck, he looked over toward the car wash. Sammie Winters was talking with one of the attendants, a young man unfamiliar to Father Frank.

He judged the boy to be about five-eleven, maybe a hundred and seventy-five pounds, probably nineteen or twenty years old. He had black, wavy hair, and generally nice features.

Without making a conscious decision to do so, Father Frank walked over to where the two young men were talking.

"Hi, Sammie. How are things going?"

Sammie looked around with a start. "Oh. Hi, Father."

He fidgeted with a piece of string he was holding, clearly not happy about Father Frank's arrival on the scene. The boy cut his eyes to see how the other man was reacting to the priest's arrival.

"Are you working here at the car wash?" Father Frank asked Sammie.

"Naw. Just..."

When he didn't finish the sentence, Father Frank said, "Visiting your friend." He turned to the other man. "And you are?"

"A friend of Sammie's."

Father Frank pressed his lips together, nodded, and turned back to Sammie. "Would you like to introduce me to your friend?"

Sammie's eyes darted between his friend and Father Frank. His breathing became a bit more labored, and he wound the string around his thumb. He swallowed.

"Father, this is Ward. Ward, this is Father Frank."

"Hello, Ward." The priest held his hand out.

Ward ignored the proffered hand. He turned his head slightly and spat on the ground.

"And you work here, Ward?" Father Frank asked.

"That's pretty obvious, wouldn't you say, Frank?"

The priest recognized the disdain in Ward's voice and attitude. Ward looked at the priest with wary eyes, his expression sullen. Father Frank had not challenged Ward, nor asked any prying questions, but the boy's guard stood firmly in place, shielding him from outsiders.

For several moments, the three stood there, no one saying a word, Father Frank trying to understand the two boys, Ward angry, and Sammie uncomfortable.

"Well," Father Frank said. "I'll let you two get back to your conversation. Nice to meet you, Ward."

"Yeah, I'm sure." Ward barely opened his lips.

On the drive back to the rectory, Father Frank thought about his encounter with B.D. today. When it had become clear he would get no information out of the boy, Father Frank had left him standing in the woods. Twice, the priest looked back to see if B.D. was moving, or if he had picked up his knife. The second time, the boy was sitting on the ground, staring into space.

No doubt B.D. was on something, maybe drugs, maybe alcohol. Probably both. In his close encounter, Father Frank had noted the smell of alcohol, yet it didn't seem strong enough to account for the boy's demeanor. So, what *was* behind it?

One guess would be drugs but Father Frank was not experienced enough to say for certain.

The young man had denied slashing Father Frank's tires. The priest decided the boy was telling the truth about the tires. B.D. thought Father Frank had a truck because that's what he was driving today. The way that little piece of information fell into the dialog convinced the priest that B.D. didn't slash the tires.

The young man also claimed he didn't know anything about the fires. What did Father Frank expect an arsonist to do? Hop up and say, "Yeah, I'm the one who burned the churches?"

Of course B.D. denied it. But did he do it? Father Frank didn't have a clue. When B.D. thought Father Frank was after him about the tires, the boy was belligerent. When Father Frank pressed him on the fires, B.D. suddenly became afraid.

He knows something about the church fires. But what? Did he set them? Was he a member of a gang that got a high out of starting big fires? Or maybe he just knew who did.

Any one of those cases could account for the fear. Fear of being caught, either by the police, or by the arsonist.

Father Frank's thoughts switched to Ward, who showed no indication of drugs, or alcohol for that matter. Anger was his controlling force. What could cause such anger in a person that young? Whatever it was, Father Frank bet it had to do with an adult. Fights and problems between teenagers produced a different kind of anger, generally not as deep-seated, more on the surface. To have gained such control, Ward's anger must have been with him a long time. But it wasn't likely that the anger was directed at a church, and certainly not two churches.

Then there was Earl. He had threatened to run over Father Frank with his Trans-Am, and the priest had no doubt Earl was capable of carrying out such a threat. Like Ward, his eyes were the dominant features. Ward had troubled eyes, while Earl's eyes probed into a person, looking for any weakness, attacking it, and all the while, holding the person captive with their intensity.

Earl was just plain frightening. Father Frank could well imagine how Earl could influence a teenager. And he seemed to turn up in all the wrong places—the fires, The Corral, the basket-ball league, always trolling the streets as if looking for the next fish to sink his barbed hooks into. Father Frank shook his head. Earl worried him.

The Corral. That thought brought back the image of the man burning a cross. It was only two pieces of napkin but the symbol was clear. Father Frank found the most worrying aspect of the incident was the man's glee at his stunt. The priest had no idea who the man was, but the man certainly knew that Father Frank was a minister of God.

As he turned into his driveway, his mind flicked through the images of each man, like a slide show, or some virtual police lineup.

Did any of them have anything to do with the church fires? And what could be their motives? Both fires were Baptist churches. Was that relevant? Could someone blame a Baptist Church for his failed life and strike out at all Baptist Churches?

Father Frank brought the truck to a stop and got out. Questions. He had plenty of questions and not a single answer. He closed the truck door, which brought to mind the reason he was driving Mr. Zimmerman's truck today. Four slashed tires. More questions.

Was there any connection between the fires and his slashed tires? Those acts were so far apart in severity, he had to think they were not connected. Was the tire-slashing directed at him, personally, or at Prince of Peace?

He tried to think of anyone he might have made mad—mad enough to resort to vandalism. No one came to mind. If it was an attack on Prince of Peace, what was the motive there? Maybe the same as for the fires. Maybe the count stood at two Baptist Churches and one Catholic church. So far.

As he walked into the rectory, Father Frank said a prayer that whoever was burning churches would have a change of heart.

Please, God, forgive that person.

Abruptly, Father Frank stopped. What if Prince of Peace had been burned to the ground? Would he be able to forgive the arsonist?

Instinctively, he said yes, of course. But an image of his church reduced to a pile of ashes brought doubt to his mind. The focus of his prayers changed.

Dear God, help me to be kind and helpful to my fellow man, and to forgive his shortcomings, even as I hope you will forgive mine.

~ Chapter Eleven ~

Once again, Father Frank sat in the dark quiet of the confessional, waiting to help people make peace with the Lord. While he waited, he thought about his own life, and ways he could improve in God's view.

Was he spending too much of his efforts with the youth programs? No. They were the future. And they faced so many pitfalls during their teenage years. He needed to find more ways to help the youth avoid falling into those dangers, and to help them build a closer relationship with Jesus. Still, he needed to work in more time for the older parishioners. They had less time left to do God's work.

Were his sermons reaching anybody? He tried to make them relevant and interesting. He hoped each Sunday he could embed one morsel that would stick in the minds of his parishioners, and be a good influence. But did he ever succeed? It was hard to tell. He wished more people came to tell him a particular sermon had spoken to them, helped them with a problem, or encouraged them to spend more time in private conversation with the Lord.

Of course, a few always told him they appreciated his words. How about some new people? Just one new person a week. Or two. That would make a hundred additional souls he had reached during a year. Was that just pride wanting praise?

Let my words convey Your message, Lord. I don't need to be complimented; just let the parishioners grow closer to You.

The door opened, and he heard the wooden kneeler scrape on the floor as someone bowed before God.

"Bless me, Father, for I have sinned."

Father Frank caught his breath. It was Sammie. The priest felt a chill run down his back. What would Sammie have to say today? Maybe just that he had been uncharitable to someone. For the first time in his priesthood, he feared what he might hear. Father Frank felt an urge to cover his ears and just give absolution. But he knew he could not do that. He had to fulfill his part of the sacrament.

"Yes, my son."

"Father, there's gonna be another fire." Sammie's soft voice carried heavy emotions—guilt, regret, fear.

The words physically shook the priest, his stomach cramped as he tried to breathe. At the same time, the despair in Sammie's voice made Father Frank want to cry.

Somehow, though he wouldn't acknowledge it, he had expected this. The moment he recognized the penitent was Sammie, the question crept into the back of his mind. Will another church be torched?

Please, God, let me help this troubled soul.

"Have you told the police?"

He heard the boy let out a sigh. "I can't."

"You must, S—." He caught himself just before he said Sammie's name. It was difficult enough for the boy to come into the confessional and tell what he knew. He had to have at least the illusion of anonymity.

"At this point, you've done nothing wrong. If you don't tell the proper authorities, then you will have committed a sin of omission."

Quiet. And then, "I know it's a sin. I'm asking God to forgive me."

"He will. But He would like to know you are sorry for what you did. The best way to show that is to correct your wrong, to change the way you act. In this case, that means to tell the police. Then, maybe they can prevent the tragedy of another fire."

The priest paused a moment, afraid to ask, desperately wanting to know, but fearful of the answer.

"Will it be another church? Another house of the Lord?"

A chill settled over the priest. Part of him didn't want an answer. Maybe if he didn't hear, it wouldn't happen.

"Yes." Sammie spoke so softly Father Frank almost missed it.

"I'm guessing it's the same person who's burning all the churches." Father Frank waited, but Sammie said nothing. "Do you know why he's burning churches? Does he have some grievance with the churches he burns? Or with *all* churches?"

Still the boy remained silent. Father Frank wanted to yell at him, tell him this kind of loyalty was a mistake. Maybe it was fear. Maybe Sammie was afraid of the person setting the fires. Father Frank remembered the fear that appeared so strong within B.D.

"Please tell the police."

"I can't, Father. You understand that. You can't tell what you hear in confession."

Father Frank started to say that was different. But he didn't. Everyone thought his situation was unique.

"Will you meet me outside of the confessional? Tell me what you know, whatever you can, but outside the Sacrament of Reconciliation. Then, I can go to the police. You won't have to. No one needs to know anything came from you. I won't mention your name to them, or tell them how I know anything. I promise you that."

The priest heard the door open. "I can't."

Again, so soft it might have been a far-off whisper, carried in by the wind. The door closed. Sammie was gone.

Father Frank scooted his chair back and started to rise. He could go out, *accidentally* run into Sammie. Talk to him. See what he might pry out of the boy.

He sank back down. He couldn't do that. He could not give any indication he knew who was on the other side of the screen, not to the person there, not to the police, not to anyone.

And yet, Father Frank now knew another church would be burned. Another house of the Lord would be reduced to a pile of smoldering ashes. He found it physically difficult to sit still, not to take any action. But what action could he take? The laws of the Church were very clear and very strict. The seal of confession was sacred.

It had been many years since Frank Deluca had been on the verge of tears. Right now, with his hands—worse yet, his tongue—tied, he felt very much like crying.

Father Frank spent more than his usual forty-five minutes reading the Bible that night. Then he found Canon 21 of the Fourth Lateran Council, from 1215 A.D. and read it out loud.

"Let the priest absolutely beware that he does not by word or sign or by any manner whatever in any way betray the sinner: but if he should happen to need wiser counsel let him cautiously seek the same without any mention of person. For whoever shall dare to reveal a sin disclosed to him in the tribunal of penance we decree that he shall be not only deposed from the priestly office but that he shall also be sent into the confinement of a monastery to do perpetual penance."

He knew by heart the passage from Canon 983.1 of the *Code of Canon Law* that said, "It is a crime for a confessor in any way to betray a penitent by word or in any other manner or for any reason."

Any reason. That was unambiguous. For a moment, Father Frank thought about the punishment if he did break the seal of confession. It might be worth it if he could be sure a church would be saved. A life of prayer in a monastery was another way to serve God. But he would also be deposed from his priestly office. He could not give that up.

He sank to his knees and prayed for guidance. Conflict threatened to choke him. He needed to do something to prevent another church from being destroyed. Yet, the seal of confession prevented him from taking action on what he knew.

"But if he should happen to need wiser counsel let him cautiously seek the same without any mention of person."

Tomorrow was Sunday. He would go see Monsignor Decker. When Frank had been at UTA, feeling the call to the priesthood and at the same time the tug of the outside world, Monsignor Decker helped him sort his thoughts, his feelings, and make a decision. Looking back on it now, that seemed an easy problem.

~ CHAPTER TWELVE ~

Father Frank wondered if it was his imagination, but it certainly looked like there were more teenagers than usual at Mass today.

Could word of the POPsters singing have brought more kids in?

He looked at the youth choir and made a quick count. All twenty-eight members of the choir were present, even the five who were not Catholic. Not that he wanted to convert them, but Father Frank was happy they felt comfortable coming to Mass to sing.

The choir sang *Beautiful Savior* as the opening hymn. It was a little rough, but it made a good beginning. The first number in front of an audience for any chorus was often rocky. And these were kids, who had been practicing together only a short time.

At the offertory, the POPsters performed *Amazing Grace* with more confidence and nice harmony from the boys.

Father Frank thought it impossible for someone to listen to that and not be moved by the deep Christian message.

By the time they sang *Holy God We Praise Thy Name* for the recessional, the full harmony of the group came into its own and it was obvious to Father Frank the kids were enjoying themselves.

The priest looked out over the congregation and from the smiles on everyone's face he knew they felt the same way. Without thinking, he began to clap when the hymn ended. Within two seconds, everybody in the church had joined in the applause. Big grins covered the faces of the POPsters.

Father Frank could see they were pleased with themselves, and excited that the adults approved of their performance.

Outside, after Mass, Father Frank greeted the parishioners. Several choir members came up to ask how they did. He gave each a pat on the shoulder and congratulated them on a job well done. When Georgia came out, he pulled her aside.

"The group was fantastic."

"Weren't they? Phyllis and Roger have done a great job. I'm so proud of them." Georgia beamed like it was her birthday.

Irene and Norm Winters, with Sammie trailing behind, came over to Father Frank.

"Father, the youth choir was amazing," said Irene. "I heard they've only been working a few weeks."

"That's right."

"Sammie used to sing all the time," his mother said. She looked back at her son, who was studying the ground. "Didn't you, Sammie?"

Without looking up, the boy replied, "I've outgrown that stuff."

"Sam." Georgia addressed the boy in her teacher tone. "Look at me." She waited until Sammie had lifted his head to face her. "What does that mean, 'You've outgrown that stuff?' Adults sing all the time. I'll bet you have lots of CD's—I guess it's an I-Pod now—and probably every one of the singers on it is older than you."

"Yeah. Well, they're professionals. Not a bunch of kids playing at it."

"They didn't start out as professionals. And, Sam—" Her tone softened. "I remember hearing you sing at school. You were good. I think the POPsters could use you. Why don't you give it a try? If you don't like it, you can always quit."

Sammie glanced in the direction of his parents. His father was talking with Father Frank, but his mother was listening to him and Georgia. Sammie looked back at Georgia.

"Mom and Dad would make me stay in." He attempted to mimic his mother's voice, "If you start something, you have to finish it."

His mother's mouth dropped open. "Sammie."

Georgia put her hand on Sammie's shoulder. "You have my word, Sam. If you try it and don't want to continue, I'll talk to your parents. They won't make you continue, right, Missus Winters?"

Sammie's mother still had her head cocked and her mouth open. Her expression remained appalled, but she nodded.

Sammie didn't look convinced. "I don't know."

"Will you at least think about it?"

Hillary Lindale walked up and looked at Sammie with her playful cobalt eyes. Her tee shirt read, "Blue Eyes Tell No Lies."

"Hi, Sammie. You're missing a lot of fun not joining the choir." She flashed a smile to rival the sun, turned with a flip of her ponytail, and walked off.

Sammie's gaze followed her for several seconds. He turned back to Georgia. "I'll think about it."

"I hope you have some success with Sammie," Father Frank said to Georgia after the Winters' left.

"The POPsters will. Sam may think he's outgrown singing, but he hasn't outgrown Hillary."

"No, I think not."

"I don't blame him," Georgia said. "She's pretty, has a great personality, and—I don't know—a measure of self-aware-ness a lot of girls her age don't have."

Most of the parishioners had drifted off, and Father Frank and Georgia now stood alone. With a straight face, Father Frank asked, as casually as one might ask if it rained yesterday, "How did your date go last night?"

"Ah, dinner?"

"Your *date*."

A touch of pink crept up from Georgia's neck and invaded her face.

"It was very nice. We had a nice meal."

"And that was it? No conversation, no getting to know one another?"

The pink advanced upward on Georgia's face. "We did talk. A lot. In fact, since I know you're not going to stop grilling me, we talked for probably two hours after the meal. He's a very good conversationalist. Did you know Mike is a Catholic?"

Father Frank blinked with surprise. "Really? I'm sure he's never been to Mass since I've been here."

"No, he doesn't go to church, and hasn't for several years. He said police work has just made him too disillusioned. He's not sure if there's a lot of good in the world. And if there's not, what good is church?"

"What a shame. I hate for him—or anybody—to overlook all the good in the world. People are doing good deeds every minute of every day."

"I know. I tried to tell him that. What he sees are the bad guys. At the least, he comes in contact with people at their worst. Maybe good people who've made a mistake. He says he's arrested too many people who go to church every Sunday."

"Perhaps you can change that attitude, get him in a more positive frame of mind."

"I told him I was going to add a change in his attitude to my prayer list."

"And how did he respond to that?"

The blush reappeared. "He said I could work on his attitude Wednesday after dinner."

"Wow." Father Frank let out a loud laugh. "He's moving fast. Or you are. Maybe both of you."

She held up a hand like a crossing guard stopping traffic. "Just dinner. As Mike said, 'A person's got to eat.' We might as well eat together."

"And that's it? Could just as well be your sister for a dinner partner?"

"Okay." She put her hands up in surrender. "It was a lot more pleasant than eating alone, and a lot more pleasant than eating with one of my girlfriends. And while he doesn't have a little dimple in his chin like you do, he's still very handsome. Satisfied?"

"Are you?"

Her blush was becoming permanent. "His ... masculinity ... made the evening ..." She paused, obviously searching for the right word. "Okay, I'll say it. Exciting."

Father Frank smiled but said nothing.

"And you're right. I'm looking forward to Wednesday's dinner." Now she grinned. "To see if I can change his attitude."

Father Frank just chuckled as he turned and headed for the rectory.

It was just after two in the afternoon when Father Frank rang the doorbell on Monsignor Decker's house in Tyler.

"Frank. Come in, come in," said the Monsignor.

He led the way into the living room. With heavy exposed-wood furniture, wood paneling, coco colored carpet, and western art, the room reflected Monsignor Decker's early years growing up on a ranch.

"Have a seat. Would you like something to drink?"

"A Dr Pepper would be nice," said Father Frank as he settled into a comfortable chair.

The Monsignor returned with two drinks and sat on the leather sofa.

"I hear you've organized a summer basketball program," said the Monsignor.

"We've got forty-two playing, about half from Prince of Peace. And half a dozen men from the parish working with them."

The older man nodded. "Good. Give them something to do that's healthy and wholesome. I'd pick golf, of course. But I'm not surprised you picked basketball. I guess basketball is better. Appeals to more teenagers. Cheaper, too. Do you even have a golf course in Pine Tree?"

"Not in town. There's a nice course about five miles out toward Hickory Ridge."

"Never played there."

"How's your golf game these days?" Father Frank asked.

"Not bad. I'm breaking eighty-five now and then. Have yet to see eighty." The Monsignor shifted on the couch. "But you didn't drive down here to ask about my golf scores. What's on your mind?"

Father Frank took a long drink of his Dr Pepper, then looked his mentor in the eye and explained his dilemma. The Monsignor listened quietly, not interrupting. When Father Frank finished, Decker nodded several times, drank some of his soda, and leaned forward.

"The seal of confession is clear cut, Frank. The priest must maintain absolute secrecy about anything and everything that a person confesses. You can't reveal the contents directly or indirectly, or even act on it. There's no ambiguity about that. Even if it endangered your life, or the life of someone else, you cannot break that sacred trust. To do so would be automatic excommunication for you."

"I know that. But another house of God will be destroyed if I don't do something."

"And probably will be even if you were to tell the police what you know, which is not much. It goes without saying you cannot mention the person's name. But under no circumstance can you even tell the police you know another church will be burned. Even if you said no more than that. You can't do it."

"I know, I know."

The older priest took a deep breath and pulled on his grey beard.

"You probably suspected another church would be burned, didn't you?"

Father Frank nodded. "After the second one, yes. I suspected—feared—there would be a third."

"And the police probably expect it also," the Monsignor continued. "So, what would you be giving them even if they got this person who confessed to having some knowledge of the future burning? If he or she wouldn't tell you in confession, it's unlikely they would say anything to the police."

"But I wasn't threatening them. The police would."

"True." Monsignor Decker closed his eyes for a moment, then opened them. "I take it you believe he or she is telling the truth, as they know it."

Father Frank tilted his head and shrugged. "Can't imagine they would lie about that in confession. Why say anything if you're going to lie?"

"Okay. Let's think about this. First, you read about these fires in the paper."

"Yes."

"And you said you have actually gone to see the fires?"

"Yes." Father Frank felt a little embarrassed. "Well, the second one was only a few blocks from Prince of Peace. I thought maybe I could do something."

The Monsignor laughed. "Frank, I'm not picking on you. What I'm saying is that you have some knowledge of these fires firsthand. You said you sort of expected another church fire yourself. So, you can use what you read in the newspaper, and what you were thinking *before* the person came into the confessional."

"I almost think the person wanted me to do something."

The Monsignor leaned back in the chair and pulled on his beard for several seconds.

"Back in sixteen hundred and something, a decree came from the Holy Office saying a priest could not use any information that would displease the penitent or reveal his identity. I don't know if this opens the door to use the information that another church will be burned.

"But Frank, you really haven't learned anything from the penitent. Except to confirm your own fears, right?"

Father Frank waggled his head. "Probably true. I'm sorry he told me."

The older man laughed. "That's often the case when sitting in the confessional. Fortunately, I've developed the ability to forget almost immediately."

For several minutes, neither man said anything, absorbed in his own thoughts. With another tug on his beard, the Monsignor refocused on Father Frank.

"Do you have anybody in mind for these fires? Any suspects, as they say on TV?"

Father Frank rubbed his nose and thought for a moment. "There are three people in Pine Tree right now that I don't feel good about. No, make that four."

"Only four? How lucky." The Monsignor laughed. "Were you led to any of them by what you heard in the confessional?"

"No." He looked at the ceiling for a moment, then back at his mentor. "Actually, I don't know about one. I met him, a kid out of school named Ward, because he was talking to...to the penitent. Something about him, the deep-seated anger in his eyes, made me consider him."

"And if he had not been talking to the penitent, you would not have noticed him?"

"That's right."

"Hmmm. But the penitent is a member of your parish, right? Would you have stopped to talk with the penitent even if he or she had not confessed to knowledge of the fires?"

Father Frank considered this for a few seconds. He nodded. "Yes. I believe I would have."

"So, that meeting was ordained by the person being a member of your parish, not by the confession."

"True." Father Frank felt relieved.

"What about the other three?"

"One of them, a scary man named Earl, has been lurking around Pine Tree, particularly where teenagers congregate. I saw him at one of the fires, but he took off when I started toward him. I've also seen him at a place that appears to be a hangout for drug users. We've had a few words. I can certainly picture him setting fire to churches."

"So, no connection with the penitent."

"No. And one of the boys in the basketball league suggested the third person, another young man in his late teens, whom I suspect—based on my one encounter with him—is into drugs."

"And the fourth?"

"A man I saw at a bar. I was there trying to get an address for the young man I just mentioned. As I was leaving, this man made a cross out of paper napkins, lit a match and burned the cross. He watched me, and then laughed. I can only say it came across to me as evil. I've read in books about an evil laugh. I think that was my first time to actually hear one." Father Frank ran his hand through his hair.

"My only reason at this point for adding him to my list is just the burning of the paper cross. And his laugh."

"Again, no connection with the confession. So, it seems to me that you can work on this based on your belief, *before* the confession, that there would be another fire, and one of the four people you have on your list could possibly be connected."

Father Frank smiled. "Of course, I don't know what I can do with it anyway."

The Monsignor got up, signaling the end of the session. "However, let me emphasize. You cannot allow, to the penitent or to anyone else, even the *impression* that any knowledge you gained in the confessional has led you or helped you. If such an impression could come from your actions, *even* if that impression were false, then you must stop. This is a case where even the impression of wrong is forbidden."

Father Frank's mind whirled with conflicting thoughts. He could use information not gained from the confessional. But where did that lead him? And he must avoid even the impression of a break, or even a crack, in the seal of confession.

At the door, the Monsignor closed his eyes and tugged on his beard once more, apparently deep in thought. When he opened his eyes, he looked straight at Father Frank for a moment, and then opened the door.

"My final comment is, leave it to the police. You're playing with fire."

~ Chapter Thirteen ~

The Pine Tree Police Department was housed in a one-story red brick building huddled next to the town hall. On Monday morning virtually nothing was happening. Father Frank found Mike with his feet propped on the desk. The detective scrambled up to clear a stack of papers from a chair for the priest to sit in.

Documents, pieces of evidence in plastic bags, manuals, and three sacks from the local Dairy Queen covered every horizontal surface. A large white board filled most of the wall behind Mike's desk. On it were columns identified by what Father Frank assumed to be case numbers. Various pieces of information had been scrawled under the headings, some in black, some in red and blue, and a couple of items were circled in green. Several pieces of paper were held to the board by magnets.

Father Frank found it impossible to make sense of any of it, nor to decipher much of the police shorthand written on the board.

"Why are you asking about Ward Campo?" Mike asked.

Father Frank didn't have a good answer. A sudden uneasiness in his gut? A look in the boy's eyes? Those wouldn't mean anything to the detective. Father Frank couldn't say Ward was talking with Sammie, who told me in confession he knew about the fires.

"I met him Saturday. He seemed to be carrying a lot of anger. I just wondered if you could tell me anything about him."

"Is he a member of Prince of Peace?"

"No." The priest twisted in the chair, trying to find a more comfortable position. It did no good. He realized it was the questioning that made him uncomfortable, not the chair.

"So, he's not your problem."

"I'm interested in all the youth of Pine Tree. And incidentally, he is friends with some of my guys, so I'm doubly interested."

Mike leaned back in his chair and studied the priest before answering. "I can say that we have never arrested Ward Campo, nor had any occasion to. Had no complaints against him."

"But you are aware of him, apparently."

"Yes. But then, we're aware of you."

Father Frank nodded. "Point taken. And you aren't going to tell me anymore about him."

Mike just smiled.

"How about B.D. Rake?" Father Frank asked.

"Another friend of one of your parishioners?"

The detective picked up a wooden pencil and held it, one index finger on the point, the other on the eraser.

"Some of them know him."

"Well, we've had more encounters with him. He's on the edge of the drug scene. Abuses alcohol. Some other petty stuff. Never been in jail."

He moved his left index finger up and down, wiggling the pencil.

Father Frank sat silent, idly looking at the board with all the cases on it, wondering if he should mention the man from The Corral.

He debated with himself and started to let it go. Mike had enough to worry about. But just then, his eyes picked out something on the board he could actually decipher: "Cal. Rd. Bap." And below it, the word "diesel."

"I was out at The Corral the other day —"

"Whoa. I can't see that as one of your places of recreation." He slapped the pencil back on the desk. "Did I forget to tell you to leave police business to the police?"

"You did. Now, as I was saying before I was interrupted, a man made a cross out of napkins. He waited until he had my attention, then struck a match and burned the paper cross."

"You're sure he did this for your benefit?"

Father Frank nodded. "Oh yes. Quite clearly. And after it burned, he laughed a rather nasty laugh, all the while staring at me, watching to see my reaction."

Father Frank studied Mike to see *his* reaction. In true police fashion, he showed nothing.

"No doubt in my mind, it was meant for me. I felt it was a message."

Mike looked down at his desk and compressed his lips. He refocused on the priest.

"First, I'd suggest staying away from The Corral. It's not a nice place. Second, leave police business to the police."

"Ah, you didn't forget this time."

"And third, what did the guy look like?"

Father Frank smiled. "He was a big man, about six feet tall and probably needed a five foot belt. I'm not a good judge of age, but my guess is forty to forty-five. He had a droopy mustache and thinning hair. Brown. Dirty. Oh, and he had tattoos on both forearms. Some sort of designs. I didn't notice any words."

Father Frank stretched his lips into a long straight line and raised his eyebrows.

"That's the best I can do. I'd be happy to go out there with you and point out the guy, if he's there."

"No." Mike said it with finality. "There is nothing illegal about burning a paper napkin, as long as it doesn't start a larger fire. But I'll see if we have anything on a man that fits your description."

"What about Earl? You find anything about him?"

"Not much. Actually, nothing. The car is properly registered to someone else. We called the guy. He said Earl was using his car, with his permission. Wanted to know if Earl had been speeding or anything. When I asked him what Earl's last name was, he said Earl was all he knew.

"I challenged him on that. I mean, he's loaned his car to someone and doesn't know his last name? I don't think so. He said, 'Sorry, I wasn't thinking. Smith. Earl Smith.'"

The detective shook his head and frowned. "Clearly, something's not right. But until he breaks the law, runs a red light, has a tail light burn out, anything, there's not much else we can do." Mike raised his shoulders and let them drop. "In the U.S. of A. we can't stop a person and ask for identification without a good reason."

"No last name. Sounds pretty questionable to me."

Mike leaned forward and put his elbows on the desk. "Whatever you're thinking about, forget it. The police investigate problems, solve crimes, put the bad guys in jail. You're supposed to be saving souls. Stay out of our territory and we'll stay out of yours."

"Oh, I welcome you into mine. I can use all the help I can get. Why don't you come around on Sunday morning and see how we do it?" Father Frank opened his eye wide, cocked his head to the side, smiled, and waited for a response.

"Maybe not."

Father Frank decided he wasn't going to get any more information out of Mike on this front. Maybe he should try a different one.

"How was your date Saturday night?"

A big smile replaced the frown that had taken up residence on Mike's face.

"Now *that* was okay. She's a very classy lady. Everybody turned to look at her when we entered the restaurant."

"So, I'm thinking it won't be many days until you do it again." Father Frank grinned, knowing that Mike had asked Georgia out for Wednesday night.

"Well, a guy's gotta' eat. And I can't think of anyone more pleasant to eat with than the Georgia peach."

"The Georgia peach." The priest laughed out loud.

"Hard to argue with that. I know, I know. I'm sure she's gotten that many times over the years."

Father Frank stuck his index finger up. "Maybe not. Remember, she wasn't a Peitz until she married Leo, after she was out of college, well past the teasing years."

Mike turned serious. "We had a very nice evening. We talked for a long time. I can't remember ever talking to a woman for that long at one time. Well, I never did. But it was easy with Georgia. I hated to quit."

"So, you liked it. How about Georgia?"

A deep worry line etched across his brow. "I think so. But maybe I'm just wishing. She seemed...well, she smiled a lot."

"Georgia always smiles."

Father Frank felt a little mean giving Mike a hard time. But it was fun seeing the tough detective show a softer side.

"Yeah." Mike looked down a second, then raised his head with a smile on his face. "But she's going to have dinner with me again Wednesday. That says something, doesn't it?"

Father Frank got up and headed out the door. Over his shoulder, he said, "A gal's got to eat."

~ CHAPTER FOURTEEN ~

Father Frank arrived at the basketball court in time to see the end of a game where the Bears lost by one point. He clapped his hands and yelled at the kids.

"Great game, all of you. Do you realize that is the fifth game this round that has been decided by one or two points? Great competition."

Out of the corner of his eye, he perceived a giant, black tarantula turn the corner and creep along the street, looking for victims. Father Frank left the court and started jogging toward the Trans-Am, intending to confront Earl, regardless of the consequences. But before he had covered a hundred feet, the black car took off.

Father Frank came to a halt, a scowl covering his face. For several seconds, he stood there, shaking his head and clenching his teeth, frustration dominating his emotions. He turned and headed back to the basketball court.

At least he's gone. For now, anyway.

With play stopped between games, Father Frank called the guys over. "I see the black Trans-Am is still with us. Any of you guys ever talk with Earl, the guy who drives it?"

A few nods but mostly just heads down, studying the ground.

Carlos spoke up. "Like I said the other day, he asks about drugs, where he can buy some, who sells the stuff. He got angry the other day. Man, he is one scary dude."

"What'd he get angry about?"

"Said we had to know something, and we just wasn't telling him. I said no, man. None of us was into that stuff. He finally went away."

"Okay. Anybody know a Ward Campo?"

A skinny kid with about five black whiskers sticking out from his chin spoke up. "I knew Ward a few years ago. I mean, I used to see him around. But he never said much. Always looked mad. I just stayed clear of the dude. That's all I know."

"He was four or five years ahead of me in school," said another boy. "I think he dropped out before he graduated. Never played any sports or anything. I didn't really know him. I think he was in my brother's class."

"Your brother still in town?" asked the priest.

"Naw. He's in the army, up at Fort Sill in Oklahoma right now."

"Anybody else?"

The boys shook their heads.

"Better off not knowing him," said the thin kid with the whiskers.

"You should have come over and had your picture taken with the POPsters," Phyllis said to Georgia.

"No, no. It's your group. And Roger's. I haven't had anything to do with it. I mean, I've done a few things you asked me to. But you and Roger make it work."

"Well, I don't agree with that. If it hadn't been for you, we'd never have done the Sunday Mass sing."

Georgia shook her head. "You made it happen, Phyllis. And don't forget that. Sunday did go well, didn't it?"

Phyllis grinned like a kid with a new bicycle. "Yeah. It was great."

"So, have you set a date for the POPsters' first concert open to the public?"

"I haven't thought about that at all. I mean, Mass at Prince of Peace is one thing. General public? I don't know."

"Sure you do. It will be good for the kids. They like to perform. This will give them a chance to invite all their friends who don't go to Prince of Peace."

Phyllis frowned.

"What are you worried about?" asked Georgia.

"Lots of things. Who will come? I mean, what if we have a concert and only you, me and Roger show up?"

Georgia laughed out loud. "Phyllis, you are a riot. How many people would you like to have?"

Phyllis made a face. "I don't know."

"A hundred? Two hundred?"

"A hundred would be nice."

"Okay. Let's see, there are fifty-six parents. That's a sure thing. You could sell those tickets without even having a date set. Plus probably at least fifteen or twenty siblings, but we'll count only sixteen. I think those go in the category of sure thing, also. The parents will insist, even if the kids don't want to hear their sister or brother. We're up to seventy-two already. Now, if each member of the choir gets only two friends to come...Is two friends reasonable?"

Phyllis nodded. "Yeah, I would think so."

"Oops, we've gone over. That's one twenty eight."

"But where would we have it? The hall here isn't big enough for that many people."

"How about the Pine Tree Civic Center? It will hold 200 easily, probably more. It has a nice stage, not too big, but big enough, and a good sound system. It'll be perfect."

Again, worry lines formed on Phyllis's forehead. "But that costs at least a hundred dollars to rent. Probably one fifty."

"Let's see. The parents will pay five dollars each and consider it a bargain—which it is. And the kids will pay two dollars and never look back. That's four hundred and twenty-four. I'll bet we can get the Civic Center for a hundred, spend fifty on posters, leaving two hundred, seventy-four for decorations or whatever."

Phyllis was still not convinced. "How will we get the word out?"

"The fifty bucks will pay for a lot of posters and flyers if we print them on the parish computer. The kids can put up posters all over town, and hand out flyers to all their friends. I'll write up some press releases for the paper, radio, and the local cable TV."

"Won't the cable cost a fortune?"

Georgia shook her head. "Nada. Zero. Nothing. Zilch. Zip. They have to run a certain number of public service announcements. We'll give them some copy and they'll run it for a week for free. We can get Father Frank to announce it at Sunday Mass, even put it in the bulletin." She held up her finger. "The kids will know all the teenage clubs. The basketball league—that's probably fifty boys who will want to come watch the girls. Maybe the Civic Center won't be large enough."

"When would we do it?"

Georgia opened her eyes wide and tried to look totally lost. "Phyllis, this is your show. You tell me when we'll have it and I'll help you. Just tell me what to do."

"What if we're not ready? The POPsters, I mean. What if they're not ready?"

Georgia shook her head. "Not your worry. That's the director's problem. You give him a date and unless he says they can't be ready by then, he'll have them ready. You run the show, but Roger prepares the singers. See how easy it is?"

Phyllis furrowed her brows and closed her eyes for a minute. "I'll discuss it with Roger. We'll let you know on a date at practice Thursday."

"Great idea. And remember, I'll help you any way you want me to. Just tell me what you need."

Phyllis was all smiles now. "The kids are going to love this. They really enjoyed singing Sunday. This will be even better. They can invite all their friends. I'll talk to Roger about it tonight."

"Detective Mike Oakley."

"Mike, this if Father Frank."

"Good to hear from you Father. Let's see, it's been over three hours since I spoke with you. What's up?"

"Can you get me Ward Campo's address? I can't find a listing for him in the phone book, or on the Internet. And nobody around here knows."

Mike let out a long breath. "Forget it. And I don't mean 'forget it' like I'm not going to do it—which I'm not. I mean 'forget it' as in put it out of your mind. Stay out of it, Father. Do I have to bring you in on a charge of interfering with an investigation?"

"I'm not interfering. I'm looking at things you aren't."

"And just how do you know what I'm looking at? I'm telling you, stay out of it."

The receiver banged down.

Midnight had come and gone by the time Father Frank picked up his Bible and ran his hands over the rough, pebbled finish.

A good way to end a good day, he thought. *The basketball league is running smoothly. The boys are enjoying it and it gives them an activity that isn't likely to cause them any problems. Thank you, Lord. And Phyllis called to tell me the POPsters are planning a concert for the public. The youth choir provides another summer activity, keeping the kids occupied with a wholesome activity. I'm so pleased to see Phyllis growing, handling things better than I've ever seen her do before. Of course, we have to give Georgia credit for that, Lord. She has a way of getting people to move in the right direction, without getting in their way, or taking any credit for it. She must be great in the classroom. Thanks, Lord, for keeping an eye on things for us.*

He opened the Bible, flipping through the pages, looking for the passage he wanted to start with tonight. "Ah, here it is, Jeremiah twenty-three. *Woe to the shepherds who are destroying and scattering the sheep of My pasture! declares the Lord".*

Suddenly, he stopped. He cocked his head to one side, trying to hear more clearly. A siren. It could be an ambulance, taking an expectant mother to the hospital, doing its part to bring a new life into the world.

Now, a second siren. He set the Bible down, walked to the front door and went out on the porch. The sirens were clearer now, but they seemed to be heading away from him, getting softer. He scanned the hundred and eighty degrees he could see. No sign of flames. Not even a glow on the horizon.

Overhead, stars glittered brightly against a black sky. The heat of the day had dwindled to pleasant warmth. The tops of the tall pine trees near the road rocked gently. It was a peaceful night. Except for the sirens. He walked around to the back of the house, looking for any clue to the cause of the sirens.

Another plaintive scream from a vehicle joined the other two sirens. No ambulance heading for the hospital. At this time of night, it would not be police cars in a high speed car chase. Not in Pine Tree. Only two patrol cars prowled the streets after midnight.

The sirens screamed from fire trucks.

Father Frank ran into the house and called the fire department.

"Hello, this is Father Frank from Prince of Peace Church. Have you sent trucks out to a fire?"

"Yes, sir. We are responding to a fire."

"Can you tell me where the fire is?"

"No, sir. I am not allowed to give out that information."

The priest bit his lip. "Can you tell me if it's a church?"

"No, sir. I can only tell you that we are responding to a reported fire."

Father Frank hung up. What to do? His sense was the fire was west of him. But there were many churches in that direction, too many to check. Should he just drive around and look?

He checked his watch. It was too late to call. He picked up the telephone.

"Hi, Diane, this is Father Frank. I know I shouldn't be calling at this time, but has Bobby John been called out on a fire?"

Diane and Bobby John Ramsey were the first two people he had met when he came to Prince of Peace. Both taught in the Pine Tree schools, Diane in elementary school and Bobby John at the high school. Bobby John also served as a volunteer firefighter.

"Yes, Father, he has. So naturally, I'm up. You didn't wake me."

"Did he happen to say where it was? The fire." Father Frank unconsciously held his breath, waiting for her answer.

"A church. I wasn't paying attention, still half asleep. I think he said a new church."

Father Frank's mind raced. A new church. Where was there a new church in the area, one the Pine Tree Volunteer Fire Department would respond to? He could think of none. A new church. Where?

"Is that all you needed, Father?"

"Yes. Thanks." He started to put the phone down, but yanked it back up. "Are you still there?"

"Yes."

"Did he maybe say New Beginning Baptist Church?"

The fingers of his left hand tapped on the table, keeping time with his racing heart. His right hand clenched and un-clenched around the receiver.

"Yes. Yes, that was it. New Beginning."

"Thanks." Father Frank dropped the phone into its cradle, and raced for the door.

~ CHAPTER FIFTEEN ~

Why are you doing this? he asked himself. *You can't help. You'll only get in the way.*

But he could not keep himself from going. Another church. Another House of the Lord. Another place of worship.

He sped along the deserted streets and turned south on Elm Street. Immediately, he slammed on the brakes, backed into a driveway, and reversed directions.

"Pay attention," he scolded himself.

Three blocks later, he made a right turn. Now he could see the sky tinted orange behind the trees.

Again he found himself praying for another church, another set of parishioners, another minister.

God, please don't punish those who dedicate their lives to following the teachings of Your Son. Let their church be saved.

Unbidden, a passage from The Gospel of John flashed in Father Frank's mind. "In the world ye shall have tribulation, but be of good cheer; I have overcome the world."

Dear Lord, this may be part of your grand plan. But if it is an act of man, railing against Your churches, please let him find the true path, to honor your Son, not destroy His churches.

Rounding a curve in the road, he saw the flames, serpents' tongues darting out from the roof, aiming for the steeple. Tiny embers floated out, got caught in the updraft and swirled around and up, then drifted away from the inferno. If it were possible to forget about the church burning, the flying, glowing cinders, shining against the night sky looked like fireflies, darting in and about, or miniature butterflies with glowing wings.

He pulled to a stop and leaned on the steering wheel, his energy sucked away by the inferno, by the utter waste. A small explosion erupted inside the burning building, sending thousands of tiny orange rockets in all directions.

"Get back. Get back," yelled the fire chief.

Most of the men were running even before the order, shouting to others. Some, with heavy hoses, backed away more slowly, keeping a heavy stream of water aimed at the flames. One volunteer tripped over a hose and sprawled in the gravel. He jumped up quickly, blood streaming from his hand.

When no more explosions occurred in the next few minutes, the Fire Chief urged his men to move back in and attack the inferno. But even that brief pullback seemed to have encouraged the fire, its flames dancing along the ridge of the roof, covering the entire length of the building.

Finally, Father Frank forced himself out of the car. By now, thirty or forty people had arrived, most of them huddled in small groups. They talked in hushed tones, except for one group that appeared to be young men with no apparent interest in the church but only in the excitement of a big fire in the middle of the night. A photographer snapped several pictures, moved, snapped some more. After a dozen shots, he returned to his car and left.

Father Frank recognized one of the players in the basketball league. The boy stood beside two adults, probably his parents. The woman cried softly, muffled by the tissue she held to her face. The man stood, one arm around the woman, his shoulders slumped. He was looking at the fire, slowly shaking his head.

A woman in the group to his left sounded more angry than sad. She demanded to know how such a thing could happen. Why didn't the church have a night watchman? A man—apparently not her husband, as he called her Mrs. Grayson—told her the church could not afford a night watchman.

To which she replied, "Would he have cost more than a new church building?"

It was the sound that caught Father Frank's attention, a low growl. The black Trans-Am lurked under a tree, its deep-throated motor grating on the priest's raw nerves, inflaming his anger. He ran over to the car and slapped his hand on the hood, daring Earl to run him down. Instead, the Trans-Am pulled back slowly and once away from Father Frank, more rapidly. In one quick maneuver, Earl swung the rear of the car around, and without stopping, moved out forward and drove away.

Father Frank stood there, his heart still pounding, his breathing still accelerated, his anger still dominant. He took several deep breaths. He should not let Earl affect him so strongly.

He waited until his breathing returned to normal, then turned back to the fire. The firemen were losing the battle. The church was lost. Half of the crew now worked to save the adjacent Sunday school building.

Father Frank could see the strain the fire was putting on the men. Their feet dragged. They held the hoses a little lower. The commands sounded less crisp. Perhaps it was not just this fire, but rather an accumulation of three church fires in a short period of time.

To his right, he spotted Mike, standing with a uniformed policeman, well away from the fire. Father Frank dragged himself over.

"Any idea how it started?" he asked.

Mike turned. "Oh, hello Father. No. Not yet. Until they get the fire completely out, they can't get in and see what caused it."

"How'd it get called in?"

"Man down the road got up to go to the bathroom and saw it. By the time the first fire truck got here, it was fully involved. No chance of saving it." Mike's expression changed from tired to wary. "Why are you here?"

"Heard the sirens. Afraid it was another church."

Father Frank noticed Mike didn't ask how he knew where the fire was. And Father Frank didn't tell.

For another thirty minutes, Father Frank, Mike, and others watched the firemen, many near exhaustion, protect the other church building, plus two nearby houses, and work to extinguish the smoldering ember that had once been the New Beginning Baptist Church.

With the fire out, the only illumination came from the powerful floodlights of the fire trucks. Long shadows fanned out from the few remaining pieces of the church still standing. Ashes formed Rorschach patterns on the puddles of water, motionless in the windless night.

Weary fireman, faces streaked with soot, tromped through the mud and water, looking for hot spots that could reignite.

The level of urgency, and noise, dwindled. The stress and exigency that accompanied orders earlier were replaced with fatigued firmness. Only a low rumble came from the pumps on the trucks, their heavy work finished. Even the noise of the spectators, whose numbers had reached fifty or more, had dwindled with fewer than a dozen still watching.

They were undoubtedly members of the church, since they were all huddled around Reverend Jilsak, the minister of New Beginning Baptist. Upon arrival, Father Frank had conveyed his sympathy and an offer of help to Reverend Jilsak. But Jilsak was so distraught, he simply mumbled a thank you and said he would call Father Frank in a day or two.

Slowly, more of the onlookers gave up the watch and headed home. Father Frank got in his car and started for Prince of Peace. Again, he wondered about the choice of target. Another Baptist church. Three in a row. What could possibly be the motive for burning three Baptist churches? It seemed highly unlikely someone had a grievance against three churches.

Instead of turning onto Elm, he continued straight and pulled into the all-night convenience center. He picked up two cups of coffee, and returned to the site of this latest fire.

A little after three a.m., the fire chief was able to explore some of the charred remains of the church. He had made his way into what was once the entry hall, when he called Mike to come over. Father Frank started to follow, but the detective told him to stay where he was. It was still dangerous, still hot, and it *was* a crime scene.

The detective and the fire chief conferred for several minutes, squatting down and inspecting something that Father Frank could not see. They were handling something, or poking at something on the floor, just out of sight for the priest.

The discussion was carried out in hushed tones and only when Mike straightened up, did Father Frank hear him say, "I'll call it in."

Mike started toward his car, and quickly Father Frank fell in step beside him.

"What did you find in there?" he asked.

"Why don't you go on home, Father? There's nothing you can do here but lose sleep. Fire's out."

"If the fire's out, what are you calling in?"

"Go home."

Father Frank stopped. "Okay, if you won't tell me, I'll go ask the fire chief."

The detective turned and put his hand up, back in police mode. "No you won't. It's a crime scene and I don't want you contaminating it. Leave. That's an order."

For a minute both men stood looking at one another. Father Frank broke the silence. Quietly, he said, "Mike, just tell me what you found. Then I'll go. It's a church. I'm involved."

Seconds passed. "I'm sure it'll be in the paper tomorrow anyway." He paused. "I shouldn't be telling you anything." He let out a long breath. "There's a body in there."

Father Frank's eyes opened wide and his mouth fell open. "A body? Who is it?"

"Too badly burned for either of us to tell. The medical examiner will have to make the ID." He sighed. "I'm not going to let you near him. So, you might as well go home."

Father Frank nodded several times. "Can you tell how he got trapped in there?"

"We don't know." Mike opened the door of his car.

"Will you tell me when you identify him?" The priest frowned. "Is it a man or a woman?"

"If you'll stop bugging me, I'll tell you when we get a positive ID."

Father Frank drove home on autopilot, his mind working through the jumble of facts he had just received. A man trapped in the fire, burned to death. Surely he had time to ask God to forgive all his sins, to open up heaven's gate to him.

Still, why couldn't he get out? Was he trying to put the fire out and got overcome by the smoke? Father Frank had heard that more people died of smoke inhalation than actual burning. Choking on smoke would probably be easier, the priest thought. Perhaps the victim was trying to save something of particular importance to the church, or the parishioners.

And how did the fire start? Was this another arson? Surely it must have been. If there was a man there and a fire started, he could have put it out, or at least called the fire department. Mike said the call came from someone living down the road. Of course, the man could have come in after the fire was raging, tried to do something—put it out or save something—and gotten trapped.

Or, Father Frank shook his head, perhaps the dead man was the arsonist. Something went wrong, he got trapped, and died in the very fire he set.

Poetic justice? Or God saying, "Enough is enough."

By the time he got back to the rectory, he had to drag himself into the house, completely exhausted, ready to collapse. Yet, his hands were clenched so tightly the car keys dug into his palms. Deep lines etched his forehead. Hundreds of people had been disenfranchised from three different churches. He decided he would forego finishing the nightly Bible reading he had started before hearing the fire trucks. He staggered to his bedroom and changed into pajamas. He thought about brushing his teeth and dismissed it, turned out the light and fell into bed.

His eyes popped open. Even in the dark, he could see an outline of the Bible sitting on his bedside table. He had the distinct feeling the Bible was looking at him.

"I'm sorry," he said, directed toward the Bible. "My eyes just can't focus enough to read tonight. Tomorrow. I promise." Father Frank's eyes closed, and within a minute, he was asleep.

~ Chapter Sixteen ~

The clock radio roared to life, hammering out a song far too upbeat for this time of the morning. Father Frank groaned and slapped at the offending noise. Hadn't he *just* gone to sleep? He rolled out of bed, wondering why he felt so terrible, and then he remembered the events of last night.

First the fire, and another church destroyed. Then, somebody killed in the fire. Accident or murder? The violence was escalating. And still no idea of a motive. At least, Father Frank had no idea. He didn't know about the police, but Mike had not said anything about a possible motive. Earl was there. But if he set the fire, and killed a man, why hang around? The answer popped into his head instantly: arrogance. Earl had plenty of that.

He made it through Mass, managed a smile for all eleven parishioners there on this Tuesday morning. He was walking back to the rectory, giving serious consideration to going back to bed, when Abbie Sanders caught up with him.

"Have you got a few minutes to talk, Father?" she asked.

He really wanted to say no. In fact, he opened his mouth to say just that, but instead, he said, "Certainly. Could it possibly be this afternoon?"

Abbie's face, already looking gloomy, sagged a bit further. "It could, Father. But it's taken four days and all my courage to ask you. I might not have the courage again."

Father Frank looked at the woman, probably in her fifties, a bit over weight, but with the pretty face she was blessed with from youth. He could believe she might burst into tears at any moment.. And while he did not relish the thought of her crying in his office, his position demanded he be available to help—when help was needed, not when it was convenient for him.

"Come on into my office." He put his hand on her elbow, ushering her toward his office in the rectory. "I'll make a pot of coffee and we can talk."

The tears had not started for fully five minutes. Father Frank mostly made soothing noises and let her talk.

"I just don't know what to do. I make his favorite foods. I listen when he has anything to say, although mostly he doesn't talk at all." She stopped to blow her nose. "He comes home from work, eats without saying a word, then sits in front of the TV until it's time to go to bed." Sobs kept her from going on.

"Remind me what his job is?"

"He sells cars."

"So, he talks to people all day, as part of his job."

Abbie sniffed and nodded.

"Maybe he's just talked out by the end of the day."

"He's sold cars for years and we used to talk."

Father Frank nodded, trying to think of what to say.

"We haven't slept in the same bed for three months." She hid her face, but the priest could see the color rising up on her neck.

Father Frank handed her a box of tissues and waited.

"I don't know what to do. The kids are all grown and live in other cities. Andy is all I've got. And I still love him." She wiped her nose and sat up a little straighter. "But I need a husband, not a roomer. I need a friend, a companion. I need someone to share a life with, not share a house."

"Would you like for me to talk to Andy? See if I can find out what the problem is?"

A wan smile appeared briefly on the woman's face. "Yes, Father. I was hoping you would do that. I'm at my wit's end. I've tried to talk to him but he just turns the TV up louder. He's cutting me out of his life. I can't live like this, Father."

Father Frank rose and walked around the desk. "I'll call him and try to talk with him as soon as possible. I'll let you know what happens."

"Thank you. Thank you. I know you can…"

Father Frank winced. He did not know if he could accomplish anything. He would try, but he knew there was only so much a priest could do. When both partners came together, the possibilities always looked better. When one partner came alone, it was often too late.

He tried to coax up an encouraging smile. "Of course, prayer may be the best thing either of us can do."

"I'll pray. You talk to Andy."

Fifteen minutes after Mrs. Sanders left, Father Frank was spooning a large blob of salsa onto his scrambled eggs when the doorbell rang.

Heavens above. I might as well be in Grand Central Station. He walked into the living room to answer the door. He raised his eyes. *Sorry, Lord. I know I'm here to serve your people.*

Mike Oakley stood there, looking bright and energetic after what, Father Frank knew, had been a long night with little sleep.

"You could invite me in, or we can stand on the porch and talk," Mike said.

"Sorry. My mind is creeping along in low gear this morning. Come on in. Would you like some coffee?"

They sat at the kitchen table, Mike drinking coffee, Father Frank eating his salsa-laden eggs.

"It's murder, anyway you cut it. We think he was dead before the fire burned him to a crisp. We won't know for sure until we get the medical examiner's report. But either way, it's murder. The fire was arson. That's a crime. So, if someone gets killed as a result, that's murder. But I'll be surprised if the M.E.'s report doesn't tell us it was murder before the arson."

"That's what—" Father Frank caught himself. He was about to say something he shouldn't. *Careful.* "Ah, confuses me. Why are you here?"

Mike picked up the coffee pot and refilled his cup. "Tell me again about the man who burned the paper cross."

"I can't tell you any more than I did yesterday."

"Refresh my memory. I didn't take notes."

"You weren't interested."

"That, too."

Father Frank repeated what he remembered about the man at The Corral. "Not much. Sorry."

"Every little bit helps. Each piece of a jigsaw puzzle is necessary to get the whole picture."

"When do you want to go out and look for him?" asked Father Frank.

Mike shook his head. "Don't even think it. We'll handle this. If I get someone that I think is worthwhile, I might let you come down and tell me if it's the same man."

Mike put his cup down and placed both his hands on the table. "Father, let me say it as clearly as possible. Leave police business to the police."

He gave the priest a hard look, and his tone softened. "It's escalated to murder. I wouldn't want to see Georgia losing her minister."

"But you came to me."

Mike nodded. "Why? Because we have no leads. We have no motive. I'm grasping at anything that remotely looks like it could tie into the arsons. And now murder."

He picked up his cup and took another gulp of coffee, then stood up. "If I'm right, and I usually am." A grin spread across his face, then vanished. "This was premeditated murder, not an accidental encounter—wrong place at the wrong time. Planned and executed. Cold-blooded. And if you think being a priest will protect you, think again. The man, or woman, behind this wouldn't care whether you were a priest, a rabbi, or a pregnant woman."

No one noticed Father Frank enter the room. He smiled to himself. Georgia held the rapt attention of a dozen ladies, explaining what they needed to do to organize the Prince of Peace Ladies Guild.

"First, you need a committee to draft a mission statement and by-laws. I'll be happy to work with this group. I've done this before. Second, you need to set up four standing committees: governance, membership, programs, and finance. Each committee needs to select a committee chairman."

"What about officers?" asked a lady on the front row.

"That will come after this first phase. By then, you will know who would make good officers," answered Georgia.

She went on for several more minutes. When she asked if anybody had any questions, they all just stared at her.

"Father, did you want to add anything?"

"No, no. You're doing great. But when you have some time, I'd like to talk to you."

"Okay." She turned back to the group. "Talk about this among yourselves for a few minutes. I'll be back in a little bit to answer any questions that have bubbled up. Then, we'll take the first steps today."

Georgia walked over to the priest and tilted her head slightly. "What's the topic?"

He glanced at the women in the room. "Let's do this outside. It's such a glorious morning."

They found a bench under a tall, Southern pine tree. Father Frank jumped right to the subject on his mind. "Georgia, you've been in the community a lot longer than I have, and know a lot about the people, have taught plenty of them. Do you know a boy, young man, named Ward Campo? I'm guessing he's about nineteen, give or take a year. Ever have him in class?"

Father Frank waited as Georgia rested her chin in her hand and closed her eyes. After a minute, she looked up.

"No, I never had him in class." She stared off into space. "I'm trying to remember. A few years after I graduated from college, I worked a while with CPS—Child Protective Services." She looked back at Father Frank. "Mostly, I just did clerical work, never counseling, although I did sit in on some sessions. What a difficult task that is. You wouldn't believe the problems young kids can be overwhelmed with."

She shook her head and looked down at the ground. "Makes you wonder how some of them ever grow up, or have any chance at a normal life."

Once again, Georgia was quiet. Father Frank decided it was best not to disrupt her thoughts. After a few seconds, she looked at the priest. "I don't know what I can tell you, what's appropriate. It's been too long for me to remember the guidelines."

"I understand. And I certainly don't want you to break a confidence, or violate any rules. Of course, you know that I won't reveal our conversation to anyone."

Georgia continued to look at her pastor. Finally, she said, "Must have been ten years ago, maybe nine. A boy named Ward came through the system. I don't remember if his last name was Campo or not, but the age and time seems about right."

"And what brought him to CPS?" the priest asked.

"He had been sexually abused."

"By his father?"

"No. I don't think they, he *or* his mother, knew who his father was. One of the mother's men friends committed the abuse. Apparently more than once."

"And his mother reported this to the police?"

Georgia just shook her head. "No. One of his teachers asked CPS to look into Ward. See what his problems were. She knew something was wrong but not what. And she could get no help or information from the mother. CPS talked with the mother. She said Ward didn't have any problems. The teacher was the problem. But CPS brought Ward in for a talk. Little by little, the story came out."

Father Frank tilted his head to the side. "Maybe the mother didn't know."

"Oh, she knew, all right. Ward eventually told the counselor that his mother knew, had actually seen it. When CPS talked to the mother again, she denied anything ever happened."

"Did the man and woman get married?"

Georgia shook her head. "Of course not. I doubt he ever had any intention of marrying the woman."

"Did the police arrest the man?"

Once again, Georgia shook her head. "The mother wouldn't admit anything. In her testimony, the man was an angel. We couldn't get Ward to agree to testify. He was scared—terrified, actually. While the authorities were still deciding how to build a case against the man, he disappeared."

"Where is the mother now?"

"Who knows? I'd guess Ward doesn't know. Or care."

"The man. Do you remember his name?" asked the priest.

"I'm not certain I ever knew his name. I knew he left. That's all."

"Did he ever come back?"

"Not to my knowledge. I can ask around."

Father Frank closed his eyes and remembered his one encounter with Ward Campo, the deep-seated anger apparent in the young man. Certainly that would be consistent with the story Georgia had just told.

"Did he, Ward, go to any church? Or have any connection with any of the churches in this area?"

Georgia tilted her head and thought a moment before answering. "I don't think so. I think CPS suggested to Ward that it might help but had no luck there. I would guess his mother never attended any church, at least during that period of her life. I hope she eventually found God. But she hadn't at that time."

So, he would have no complaint against any of the churches that were burned, the priest thought. *No motive for arson.*

"Georgia, I appreciate your telling me this. And I promise I won't reveal it to anyone."

"I know you won't." She got up. "I guess I'd better go back in and see if I can be of any assistance to these ladies. Wonder why schools don't teach a course on organization?"

Father Frank wandered over to the church, entered and knelt at the back. What did he know? What could he do? His conversation with Georgia, while giving some insight into Ward's anger, certainly didn't provide any motive for arson. Earl, his prime candidate because of his probable connection with drugs, didn't seem to have a motive either. He hadn't been in town long enough. But he turned up at the fires.

B.D. claimed to know nothing about the arsons, but Father Frank didn't believe him. To what extent he was involved remained a mystery. B.D. used drugs, Father Frank could almost guarantee that. And he knew first hand that B.D. could be violent. But where was the connection to the fires? It wasn't as if there was money to be made burning a church. One thing Father Frank did believe was that B.D. knew more than he admitted.

Then, there was the man who burned the paper cross, now on the police radar. But neither Father Frank nor Mike knew the man's name, or anything else about him.

Sammie could provide some answers. Perhaps all the answers. But he wasn't telling much. And, to Father Frank's frustration, what Sammie *did* tell, the priest couldn't use. He couldn't even direct Mike to talk to Sammie.

Is there something I can do to help stop the destruction of your churches? Father Frank prayed. He put his head on his hands, which rested on the back of the pew in front of him. He closed his eyes.

What can I do? What can I do?

He awoke with a jolt. His hands had slipped off the pew, and he barely caught himself before he fell.

Tonight, I must get more sleep.

Father Frank decided not to cook lunch but grabbed a sandwich at the Dairy Queen instead. While he was sitting there, Dan Zimmerman came in and, after ordering, slipped into the booth beside the priest.

"Thanks again for the use of your truck," said Father Frank.

Dan waved his hand in dismissal. "Glad to do it." He sighed. "Things are getting worse, it seems."

"How's that?" asked Father Frank.

"Well, we not only had a case of arson last night, but also a murder. You didn't hear?"

"Oh, yes. I did. Actually, I'm trying not to think about it. Too depressing."

"Well, you might want to be thinking about it. The way things are going, it's only a matter of time before Prince of Peace gets the torch."

The priest opened his mouth to object.

Dan held up his hand. "I'm not a pessimist. I'm a realist. Three church fires in, what, less than two weeks? The slashed tires might have been a warning, a wake-up call. Did the police find out anything about that?"

"No. At least, they haven't told me anything."

"I'd call and ask them." He stood up as the waitress called his number. "Could have been the first salvo."

Father Frank liked Dan. Right now, however, he wished Dan had chosen Subway for lunch today. The priest looked out of the window in time to see a man strike a match and place the flickering flame under his cigarette. Father Frank looked away and focused on the table top. Even a burning match gave him the willies.

He had considered the possibility of Prince of Peace getting caught in the wave of arsons. He just didn't need to be reminded of it, especially right after a person had been killed. He decided maybe a pecan fudge Blizzard might help bring him out of his depression.

Father Frank stopped at the police station and found his way to Mike's desk.

"Making any progress?"

"Not much."

Father Frank sensed a mild annoyance in the detective's tone, but he ignored it. "Dan Zimmerman said I ought to ask you if anything had turned up on the tire slashing. So, I'm asking."

"Nothing. We've got so little to go on, I don't expect to find anything. On that one, we just have to get lucky."

"Lucky?"

"Yeah. The guy tells someone, who tells someone, who tells us."

"Not too likely."

The detective rubbed his nose. "Happens. Guy has too much to drink. Or wants to brag, maybe impress some girl. Then, it's 'Did you know that Wayne slashed Father Frank's tires?' and first thing you know, it makes its way to us."

"Same thing on the fires?"

"Hasn't happened yet. With three fires, good chance there'll be some buzz out there. But so far, we haven't heard even a whisper. Right now, we're going on the theory that all three were set by the same person."

"Why?"

"Same M.O. They happen about the same time of night. They've all been started using diesel as the accelerant. All three Baptist. Even the point of origin is similar."

The priest sighed softly. "Except last night's included a victim. Have you identified the body?"

The detective nodded. "Just got it. Lab finally managed to extract some usable finger prints. Turns out, he had a few run-ins with the law. Nothing too major. But enough to get his prints on file. Joseph Josephson. Ever hear of him?"

"No."

"Went by Joe."

"Doesn't ring a bell. Where'd he live?"

"Out in the county. Road 9289. We've got one of the sheriff's guys checking on it, see if there's anybody at that address. That's about all we know."

The priest ran his tongue around his teeth, hesitant to ask his question. So, he made it into a statement instead. "I'm sure you asked Reverend Anderson if Josephson was a member of his congregation."

Mike smiled. "Of course. Believe it or not, we know what we are doing."

"So, why was he in the church?"

Mike shrugged. "Maybe he was the arsonist and stayed too long. M.E. hasn't given us cause of death yet. Probably today. When we know what he was doing in the church, we'll probably solve the case."

"How about the big guy from The Corral? The one who burned the paper cross."

"Nothing on him so far. I went out there but nobody was talking. Sent another detective out, dressed down to the place. He didn't find out anything either. Probably made him as soon as he walked in the door. I imagine after my visit, the word went out. I doubt we'll see him there again, at least not any time soon."

Father Frank thought for a minute. "I could—"

"No, you couldn't. Stay away from there. Leave this to us." He punctuated this with a definitive jerk of his head. "Now, go. I've got to get some work done."

It seemed to Father Frank that he was spending all his time being conflicted about one thing or another. Now the question was, should he call Georgia or not? In the end, he decided he had little to lose by asking her. He picked up the telephone and dialed.

"Hi, Georgia. Getting ready for your date tonight?"

"Just going to dinner."

"Still a date."

"Did you call to give me a hard time, or did you have something else in mind, Father?"

"I'm sorry. Just couldn't resist. I like both you and Mike. I hope it works out."

"Works out?" Her voice rose an octave. "This is dinner. A dinner date, if you insist. Nothing more. Now, I do have other things to do, so if you have anything else, get on with it." She was not easily cowed.

"Have you ever heard of a Joe Josephson?"

Georgia said nothing for a moment. "Not that I can remember off hand. Why?"

"That's the name of the man killed in the fire last night."

"Oh," Georgia said. "Does he, did he, live in Pine Tree?"

"No. Out in the county. I think Mike said county road 9289. They're checking to see if there's anybody there who might know him."

"Hmm. Not a member of that church?"

"No."

"I'll ask around."

"Let me know if you find out anything." He paused just a beat. "And have a good dinner tonight."

"I will—ah, let you know, if I find out anything, that is. And I won't tolerate any questions about how my dinner goes."

"I wouldn't think of asking," Father Frank said in his most innocent tone of voice.

He hung up the phone, started to get up, then sat back down. He looked up a number in the parish directory and punched in the numbers.

CHAPTER SEVENTEEN

Father Frank hung up the telephone and leaned back in his chair. He had convinced Andy Sanders to come in for a talk the next evening at six. It had not been a pleasant conversation. Andy wanted to know why Father Frank was being so pushy. The priest couldn't tell him it was at Abbie's request. That would kill any chance of success. If Andy came with a closed mind, it would be difficult to get very far.

The first task was to get Andy into the meeting. Step one accomplished. He would worry about step two tomorrow.

There had been lectures on marriage counseling at the seminary. But lectures and lessons measured up to actually doing it in much the same manner as reading an article on playing tennis measured up to getting on the court and facing an opponent. This would be only his second "real live test" of marriage counseling since he was ordained. The first case had been somewhat easier. He said a short prayer asking for guidance in his meeting with Andy.

The phone rang. *Please, not another marriage problem*, he thought.

"Prince of Peace," he answered.

"Are you a Prince?" a strange, somewhat unreal voice asked. "The Prince of Peace?"

"Ah, no. I'm not a prince, I'm the pastor—is that you, Georgia?"

Georgia giggled on the other end of the line. "For a moment, I had you going, didn't I?"

"Yes, you did. I never thought of you as mean-spirited."

"Now you know. I only do that to people who taunt me about having dates."

"I guess I deserved that. What's on your mind? You need guidance in what to wear tonight?"

"I do not. And if you're not nice to me, I won't tell you what I found out."

Father Frank held up his right hand, thumb holding down his little finger. "I promise to be nice, scout's honor."

Georgia giggled again. "Good. For how long?"

"Depends on *what* you found out."

"Well." Georgia made that a two-syllable word. "First, earlier, you'd asked about Ward. The records on Ward Campo are sealed, so we're not going to find out anything from CPS."

"Not a surprise."

"But I did find someone who had heard of Joe Josephson. Turns out, he was one of Ms. Campo's many men friends. The person I talked with couldn't be sure of the dates. After all, we're talking nine years or so. But she thought that Josephson was in the picture about the time Ward came to CPS."

Father Frank settled back in his chair. Ward, at the very least, would have known Josephson. Which, of course, meant nothing. By itself. He needed to talk with Ward.

"Would any of your numerous contacts happen to know where Ward lives?"

"I doubt it. I know when his mother was here, they lived out past the milk plant. But she's been gone for... " Father Frank could hear her sucking on her teeth. "I'm guessing, maybe three to four years, maybe five. It was on the left side of the road, not far past the plant. Not much else out there, until you get half way to Winston."

"Thanks, Georgia. And I won't even ask about your date tonight."

Father Frank sat staring into space. It wouldn't do to go knock on the door and ask if Ward Campo lived there. He had already checked the telephone book. No Campo listed, Ward or otherwise.

His eyes popped open wide and he picked up the telephone book. A few moments later, he dialed.

"Hi. Is Ward there?"

The man at the car wash said, "No. He didn't show today."

"Does he still live out past the milk plant?" Father Frank held his breath.

"Yeah. Far as I know, he ain't moved."

"Thanks."

Thirty minutes later, Father Frank sat in his car, looking at what he hoped was Ward Campo's house. In many ways, it looked like B.D.'s house, about the same size and shape. Except Ward's house had been painted in recent years and the yard was neat. No fences delineated the property. The porch had been recently rebuilt. Like B.D.'s house, there were two windows in the front. Here, both contained unbroken glass and had shades, which were pulled down. No car sat in the dirt driveway. No lights were on inside, no sound filtered out.

Father Frank got out and went to the front door and knocked. When no sound came from inside, he knocked louder.

"Ward?" No answer.

The priest looked up and down the road. The only vehicle in sight was a milk truck pulling into the plant a quarter mile to the south. He checked around the left side. Nothing there. Again, the window had a shade pulled down, allowing no suggestion of what was inside. He continued around to the back.

Like the front, it contained a door and two windows, but here, one of the windows was high, possibly into a bathroom. And the back door had glass in the top half. As with all the windows, a shade covered the glass, allowing no view inside.

A short distance behind the house, a tire swing hung from a high branch of a hickory tree. From the looks of the ground underneath, it got used frequently. As he looked at it, he realized it was higher off the ground than one might expect for a young kid.

To drag your feet under that swing, you'd have to be pretty tall, Father Frank thought. *As tall as I am.*

Farther out, a burn barrel smoldered. Ward must have been here sometime today. Father Frank walked to the barrel and looked inside. He rummaged around the immediate area until he found a piece of reinforcing rod. He picked it up and poked around inside the barrel. Tin cans, remnants of cardboard boxes, and aluminum foil pans seemed to be the bulk of what had not burned. Certainly nothing from which he could gain information, other than Ward liked TV dinners.

Father Frank started back toward the front of the house. The remaining side of the house provided no more information than the previous three had. But something in the back of his mind stopped him. He walked back and looked at the rear door again. Yes. His mind had recorded it correctly. The door used an old standard skeleton key, which meant it had a keyhole.

Probably he would be able to see nothing, but he was here, and that was his only chance to see anything. Bending down, he peered through the small keyhole.

He was looking into a tiny room. A table, probably eighteen inches square, sat in the center of the floor, with two folding chairs beside it. He couldn't see much else, but salt and pepper shakers, and an apple on the table made Father Frank believe this was the kitchen. An opening at the far side led into another room. He could see some furniture there and what looked like the front door. Probably the living room.

What captured his attention, however, what caused him to suck in air, was sitting on the floor of the kitchen. A yellow, plastic container that looked like it might hold five gallons.

Stamped on the side was the word "DIESEL."

~ CHAPTER EIGHTEEN ~

He tried the door. The knob turned but the bolt stopped it from opening.

Just as well. I shouldn't trespass.

He looked at the keyhole again. Sometimes those old locks could be picked easily. He shook his head. What was he thinking? That would be out and out wrong. But there could be some evidence inside, something that would point to Ward. Or not.

Remember, he cautioned himself, *Ward is only a suspect in your mind. As far as you know, he has done nothing.*

Father Frank took a deep breath. It made no difference. Tempting as it was, only an emergency would justify breaking into someone's home.

As he drove back into Pine Tree, he could not remove the image of the diesel can from his memory. Why would Ward Campo need diesel fuel? He didn't have a tractor.

Why couldn't he have a car that used diesel? Father Frank answered his own question. *He could.*

Mike said all three fires had been started using diesel as the accelerant. Of course, in this community, diesel was a common commodity. Many people had diesel tractors. Even more had diesel trucks.

Even if Ward had the means, did he have any motive? If, and Father Frank realized it was a big *if,* Josephson had been the man guilty of abusing Ward, what did that have to do with burning churches?

Father Frank had just passed the city limit sign, when a mud-covered truck passed him, and without warning swerved over only inches in front of the Taurus. Father Frank jerked the wheel to the right and slammed on the brakes. Instantly, the car fishtailed. With teeth clenched, he struggled to bring the car under control. His car left the pavement and the steering wheel almost wrenched free as the first tire found the softer dirt of a shallow ditch. The Taurus headed for a concrete culvert, wheels locked and skidding on slick grass. The priest had no control over the car.

Three feet from the culvert, the parish car stopped. But Father Frank's pulse still raced. He laid his head on the steering wheel, and took a series of deep breaths, trying to slow the rapid fluttering of his heart.

Suddenly, something smashed against his window. Adrenalin shot through him as his head popped up. Inches away, a red, angry face was yelling at him. Beyond the screaming man, Father Frank saw the truck that had run him off the road, sitting on the side of the road a few yards away, driver's door standing open. Carefully, he rolled the window down a third of the way.

"... hole, and don't you never do nothing like that again or I'm gonna whup your hide. Cops been after me. Why? Cause you sicced 'em on me."

Father Frank looked at the man, confused over his tirade. Then he remembered the face. The man from The Corral. The paper-cross-burning man. He was still yelling.

"Let's talk about this," began Father Frank. "What's your name?"

"None of your business."

"I told the police what you did, nothing more. You were taunting me by burning a paper cross."

"Yeah, yeah. Ain't nobody gonna back up *that* story. No one. I ought to pull you outa this piece of junk and beat your face in right now." The man turned redder with each new threat.

Father Frank's breathing and heart had slowed down, but the adrenalin was still pumping, and he was angry at being run off the road. Still, he tried to remain calm.

"In light of three churches being burned in the last ten days, what you did was uncalled for and, frankly, pretty stupid."

"Maybe them churches needed to be burned. Maybe they got what they had comin' to 'em. Maybe more of them do-gooders need to fry. Maybe *your* church'll be next, huh? How would you like that? Maybe you needs to be taught a lesson."

The man's threat to Prince of Peace was like a punch in the stomach for Father Frank.

"Shall I get out and let you try it?" He had had about enough of this yelling maniac.

The guy stood over six feet and probably outweighed the priest by fifty pounds. But as out of condition as the guy looked, Father Frank was sure he could handle the fat man. One good punch to his belly and the man would be out of it.

The man sneered. "Why don't you do that? Give me a chance to stomp your butt into the dirt."

Despite the challenge, Father Frank noticed the man continued to lean his considerable weight on the car door, making it impossible for the priest to get out.

What am I doing? I'm a man of God, supposed to promote peace and forgiveness. Turn the other cheek. I'm letting him dictate things. Not good.

"Okay. We both have gotten a little excited. Let's just back away and forget this happened."

"What I thought. Sissy priest ain't got the guts to settle it man to man. 'Fraid he'll get his pretty face messed up. Maybe you ain't even a man. You run and hide behind the cops. Next time we meet, I'm gonna put a fist in your face."

The man slapped his hand against the door, let out a roar, and stomped off. He slammed the door on his truck so hard, the glass fell out, which started him screaming and cussing again.

Father Frank carefully backed his car out of the shallow ditch and drove off as the man struggled to put the glass back in place.

~ CHAPTER NINETEEN ~

As soon as Father Frank arrived back at the rectory, he put in a call to Mike.

"The overweight man who likes to play with fire is still around," the priest said.

"You been back to The Corral?" Mike's tone of voice showed his disapproval.

"No, I did not go to The Corral." Father Frank didn't bother to say where he had been. "I was driving back into Pine Tree, on the old milk plant road, when a pickup ran me off the road. Guess who the driver was?"

"Were you hurt?"

"No. I'm fine. He forced me into a ditch, then came and yelled at me for getting the police on his case."

"In a ditch. Was your car damaged?"

"No. It's a shallow ditch just beyond the Exxon station. I was able to back out with no trouble. Far as I can tell, no damage to my car at all."

"What did he do? I want to know exactly what happened."

A loud clatter came through the telephone, and Father Frank moved the hand-set away from his head for a moment. When he pressed it to his ear again, Mike was talking.

"Sorry about that. Dropped the phone trying to get my notebook open to the right spot. Okay. What happened?"

"I was driving about the speed limit. He passed me, and cut across in front of me so sharply I had to swerve into the ditch to avoid hitting him. He jumped out of the truck and came pounding on my door."

"What kind of a truck?"

"I don't know. A big truck, extended cab. Red. Covered with mud."

"So asking for the license number is a waste of time?"

"'Fraid so. Truth is, I forgot to look. I guess I was a little keyed up."

"Okay. What'd he do next?"

Father Frank tried to reconstruct the tirade, and his responses. He ended by saying, "The important thing is, he said maybe the churches deserved it, and maybe more would fry. I think that's the word he used, fry. Said maybe my church would be next, and that would teach me a lesson."

All Father Frank heard was silence for a minute. Then Mike said, "Okay, I think I got most of that down. Do you want to come down and file a formal complaint, so when we catch up with him, we'll have more to keep him on?"

The priest thought about that for a moment. "No. No harm, no foul. My car wasn't hurt, and he didn't touch me. But his threat against Prince of Peace sounded sincere. Can you keep a closer look out for him? And patrol our area a little more?"

"Yes. I'll put out the word that this guy is still in the picture and beefing up his role. I'll get the night patrols to loop by your place more often."

"Thanks."

"I still think you ought to come down and file a formal complaint. Get it on the record."

Father Frank thought about that for a minute. "No. At least not yet."

He hung up the phone and sank down on a chair. Until he reported what the man had said, the priest hadn't given much credence to the man's ranting about Prince of Peace church being a target. Now, his stomach roiled. Father Frank remembered how he felt watching the other churches burn. He could only imagine how much worse it would be watching his own church going up in flames. Maybe he *should* have filed a police report on the incident.

Why don't I have a nice watch dog, maybe a German Shepherd? Or a pit bull.

POPsters rehearsal started at 7:00, but by 6:45 when Georgia and Phyllis arrived, almost all the teenagers were already there, chattering away.

"It's so sad," Hillary was saying to the group. "They don't have a church. They don't even have songbooks." She turned to Georgia and Phyllis. "Isn't there anything we can do to help them?"

"By 'them', do you mean one of the Baptist churches, or do you mean all three?" asked Georgia.

"I guess all three," answered Hillary.

"What did you have in mind?" Georgia's brain was already working on the problem.

"I don't know. A bake sale, maybe?"

One of the boys chimed in. "How about a raffle?"

A girl with pink ribbons in her hair said, "Why bother? Those wouldn't raise enough money to even notice. We had a cake sale at school and raised a hundred and thirty dollars. That was good for the Spanish club but wouldn't help the churches any."

For a minute, no one offered any more suggestions. Then Georgia said, "How about a benefit concert? You've already got a concert planned. Why not turn it into a benefit?"

A number of the choir members liked the idea but then the girl with the pink ribbons spoke up again.

"So we raise three hundred instead of one thirty? Still won't make any difference. And even if we fill the hall, we're not gonna make three hundred dollars after paying for stuff."

Georgia held up her hand until everyone was silent. "First, we name it a benefit concert and raise the price of tickets. Then, we get sponsors."

Hillary looked confused. "What good do sponsors do?"

"They *pay* to be sponsors," said Georgia. "And we go after the businesses in town. Get as many as possible to kick in, and we'll list them as sponsors in the program. The more they contribute, the bigger their name in the program."

Phyllis stepped forward. "We don't have a program."

"We do now," said Hillary. "I think it's a great idea. My Dad owns the tire shop. I can get him to be a sponsor."

"Won't the program cost a lot?" asked Phyllis.

The ribbon girl raised her hand. "Maybe not, Mrs. Traynor. My next door neighbor has a printing shop. I could ask him to donate the programs. I bet he'd do it. He goes to Pine Valley Baptist. He was pretty bummed when it burned. I'll ask him."

Phyllis nodded. "Okay. How many want to try this?"

A chorus of "Yeah," "Let's do it," and "Go for it," resounded in the small room.

"Can we sell enough tickets at higher prices?" she asked.

"We'll sell more'n we can get in," one of the kids yelled.

Phyllis looked at Georgia, and then back at the kids. "Can you sell enough to fill the hall two nights? Friday *and* Saturday?"

"Count on it," the kids yelled back.

Once Roger arrived and was filled in, he was as excited as the kids, and immediately started them on a new song.

"Will you help?" Phyllis asked Georgia.

"You know I will. Why don't we meet tomorrow morning and put together a plan."

~ Chapter Twenty ~

Wednesday proved uneventful, for which Father Frank was thankful. He'd had an hour to enjoy the basketball games, some uninterrupted time to start a sermon, and for the first time in two weeks, had called his mother to see how she and his dad were doing, and if they had heard anything from his brother.

"What have you heard from Tim?"

Father Frank's brother, Major Tim DeLuca, was serving his second tour of duty in Afghanistan.

"So far, so good," his mother said. "The Vice President spoke to a bunch of the troops and Tim had his picture taken with him. Tim said he didn't vote for the guy, but it was still kind of neat to have his picture taken with the Vice President of the United States."

Father Frank could hear the worry in his mother's voice. She and his Dad were proud of Tim and what he was doing. But they understood the danger.

"Remember to pray for him, Frank."

"I do every day, Mom.

Father Frank hung up and stared off into space, thinking about his big brother. They differed in many ways. Tim loved golf, an individual sport, while Frank loved basketball, definitely a team sport. Tim was married and had a happy, three year-old girl, Katie. Frank had chosen the priesthood and would never have children of his own.

A grin crept up Father Frank's face. *Tim is trying to save people's lives. My job is to help people save their souls. Maybe we're not so different after all.*

He reached for the phone, intent on calling Katie. Father Frank showered her with attention and she squealed with delight whenever Uncle Frankie called. But just as his hand touched the phone, it rang.

"I don't want to be an alarmist," Mike's voice boomed through the telephone.

"Already, I'm alarmed," said Father Frank, with a chuckle.

"Some of the guys around here and I were talking. The general consensus was you ought to leave the lights on outside the church. Not that we have any reason to believe Prince of Peace might get hit—or any other church, for that matter. But outside lights are an excellent deterrent to any kind of vandalism."

"Are you taking—"

Mike interrupted. "I'm just saying it's a good idea to leave some lights on at night. They call them 'Security Lights' for a reason."

"Gotcha. I'll start tonight."

Nighttime and darkness remained three hours away. He would have to figure out which lights would provide the most illumination on all sides. To the north of the rectory, beyond his grassy yard, was a large parking lot, bordered on the south and east with pine trees. Sam Hostenbacker owned a paving company. After this year's particularly wet and muddy spring, he had offered to pave the area, in lieu of his weekly offering for the year. Father Frank had snapped up the offer and now Prince of Peace had a beautifully paved parking lot, complete with white striping.

Unfortunately, no lighting had been installed. An oversight. Father Frank realized that his only outside lighting came from the small lights found outside each door on the church and the hall.

Our night time activities justify decent lighting of the parking area.

He sighed. He would make do with what he had. By nine o'clock, he would have those lights on, and all the church buildings locked.

Father Frank checked his watch. Ten after six and Andy Sanders had not shown up. Not that he had wanted to come at all. He had demanded to know what this was all about and when Father Frank wouldn't tell him, Andy said he would not come. In the end, the priest had convinced him to stop by, if only for a few minutes.

Now Andy was late. Was he coming at all? Father Frank was about to call Andy to remind him when the doorbell rang. Father Frank opened the door to see Andy standing there, looking like the kid called to the principal's office, his earlier belligerence gone.

"Sorry I'm late," was all he said.

Once they were seated in the office, Father Frank asked a few questions about Andy's job, his kids, and then asked, "How are things going at home?"

Immediately, Father Frank could see Andy's demeanor change from questioning to defensive.

"Things are fine. Fine."

For a long minute, neither man said anything. Finally, Father Frank said, "Are you seeing another woman?"

Andy's eyes jerked open wide, and a wry look came on his face. "Of course not. Who told you that?"

"Nobody. But your wife seems to think she's losing you. She doesn't think you're living as husband and wife, more like two roomers in the same house."

Andy looked down at the desk, but didn't say anything.

"Do you still care for Abbie?"

Andy still didn't look up. "Well, yeah."

Father Frank could see this was very difficult for Andy.

But It's not easy for me either. I'm prying into the private life of a man who doesn't want to talk to me about it. Maybe he doesn't want to talk to anybody. But the wife is an equal partner in the marriage, and she wants some help.

"How do you see the situation, Andy? Are the two of you growing apart?"

Andy looked up at the priest for a second, then back down at the desk. "Yeah. I guess we are."

"Can you think of any reason why that's happening?"

Andy studied his knees for several seconds. "Well, she has been putting on some extra pounds lately."

"Andy, have you looked at your waistline recently? I'd say you're keeping pace with her, wouldn't you?"

Andy made several quick nods.

"I know this isn't easy. Can you imagine how difficult it was for Abbie to come to me on her own. She told me things aren't going well. She's desperate. She loves you and she's afraid she's losing you." He paused a moment before continuing. "Think about this for a minute before you answer. Would you want to lose Abbie?"

As soon as he said it, Father Frank had misgivings. What if the man didn't care? What if he said that would be okay with him? But the question had to be asked. It was the answer Father Frank dreaded.

Andy waited only a few seconds before he began shaking his head. "No."

"So, what's happening? Why are you two drifting apart? Do you have any thoughts on that?"

The husband closed his eyes and let his head slump down until his chin nearly touched his chest. His head rose and fell as he breathed. Finally, he looked up at the priest.

"I don't know. We used to do all sorts of things together. And have fun doing it."

"Like what?"

"Oh, I don't know. When the kids were home, there was always lots of stuff going on. We went to Little League, and school stuff, like plays and chorus. Ginnie, that's our daughter, was in chorus and the theatre group. Ted, our son, was always in one sport or another. He was a good baseball player, great hitter. Almost got a scholarship to college. Abbie and I went to all of those things, games, plays, whatever." He hunched his shoulders.

"Now, the kids are gone. Both of 'em got job offers out of state after college. We don't get to see them but maybe once a year. Even Christmas, they spend every other year with their in-laws."

"How long have they been gone?"

"Ginnie, must be six years now. That makes five for Ted."

"But you and Abbie haven't been growing apart for five years, have you?"

"No," said Andy. "We used to play tennis. We went to movies. Sometimes we just went for a drive in the country. We used to play bridge with the O'Reilly's pretty much every week. We did lots of things." He shook his head. "Now, we never do anything. Just watch television."

"So, why did you quit? Why don't you do those things now?" asked the priest.

Andy patted his stomach. "Well, I can't get around on the tennis court anymore."

"They still show movies."

"Yeah, but most of them are pretty rotten."

"Bridge?"

"The O'Reilly's moved to Dallas."

Father Frank scratched his temple, then ran his hand over his chin.

"Why don't you call the O'Reilly's and go visit them some Saturday?"

"Saturday's a big day for me at work."

"Okay. Pick another day. Sunday afternoon. Drive into Dallas, eat lunch in a nice restaurant, visit the O'Reilly's. Maybe play some bridge. Go to a movie. Take a drive into the country. All of those things are still open for you to do. And you could go bowling instead of the tennis."

"I don't know whether Abbie would want to do that. She doesn't ride in the car as good as she used to."

"How about you? Are you willing to try some of those things?"

Andy pressed his lips together, and nodded. "Yeah. But she—."

Father Frank cut him off. "Andy, do you hear yourself? Your first response is to find an objection. There's always a problem, a reason something won't work." He stopped and stared at the man. "Tell you what. I'll bet you a hot fudge sundae that if you ask her to do *any* of those things, she'll say yes."

Andy gazed down at his stomach. "I probably don't need a hot fudge sundae." He looked up at the priest. "But I'll ask her."

"And why don't you try to think up at least one thing that you two can do together each week?" The priest put on his best angelic smile. "It might go so well, you could decide to do it more than once a week. A dinner out, just the two of you, at some nice restaurant, might improve things a lot. Are you willing to try, really make an effort?"

"Yeah, I'm willing."

"That didn't sound too convincing." Father Frank gave a short chuckle.

"Okay. Yes. I'll make the effort." Andy nodded several times.

"And, Andy, if you'll ask her out, almost like a date, I know it will make her happy."

"I'll try. I really will."

Father Frank walked around and sat on the edge of the desk next to Andy. The priest could see the defensive posture Andy had maintained earlier—arms firmly crossed over his chest signaling no intrusions allowed—was gone now. He seemed almost relieved, as if he was glad to have this put on the table. Surely he was aware of the state of his marriage. He probably saw it as inevitable, impossible to change. Now perhaps, something could be done.

Father Frank leaned close to Andy, trying to make this intimate, personal. He spoke almost in a whisper.

"Abbie's quite a woman. It took a great deal of courage for her to come." He paused. "She's desperate, Andy. In her mind, you've already left." The priest swept his hand out to the side. "You're gone." He paused again, just for a second. "And she wants you back. It's up to you to make her understand you care about her. That you love her. You two can put that spark back into your lives. She took the first step. Are you willing to take the next one?"

"Yes." He got up. "I do still love her. It's just, we've gotten in a rut. *I've* gotten in a rut. And it's boring."

Father Frank started to speak, but Andy held up his hand. "I know. I can change that. And I will. Thanks for the talk, Father. I admit I didn't want to come. I guess in the back of my mind, I was afraid Abbie was unhappy."

"She is."

"But she doesn't want to leave." For the first time since he entered the rectory, Andy smiled. "I'll ask her for a date tonight."

~ CHAPTER TWENTY-ONE ~

Georgia would never admit it to anyone but she had actually stopped at the drugstore and purchased new blush, eye shadow and mascara. Fortunately, she did not run into any of her friends while in the cosmetic department. *And why would that have embarrassed me?*

She sat in front of the mirror trying to get the effect just right. *I go in there and buy lipstick frequently.* A tiny smile curved her mouth. *But not because you're going on a date.* She stared at her reflection.

Might as well make the best of what God gave me.

Getting ready took much longer than expected. She had selected three outfits before settling on a wheat-colored linen skirt and a matching silk blouse. She dug around in the back of her closet until she found her open-toed beige shoes with one-inch heels.

Finally, she dabbed a touch of perfume behind her ears, something she had not done in three years. Now, a hank of hair was curled around a hot iron.

Mike is taller than Leo. Probably six two. And chocolate-colored eyes. That explains it. I never can resist chocolate.

A teeny smile played around the corners of her mouth as she thought about the man coming to pick her up.

The wave in his dark hair and the scar over his left eyebrow make him sort of... ruggedly handsome.

She unplugged the curling iron and put it safely aside. After trying on several necklaces, she finally chose one woven from three colors of gold, that laid flat on her skin. Leo had bought it for her to celebrate her twenty-fifth birthday.

Nine years ago. Hard to believe.

She knew Leo would approve of her wearing it on a date.

She spent several minutes inspecting herself in the mirror before pronouncing herself ready. Mike said he'd taken his first job as a policeman at twenty-three. And later, he said he had been on the police force nine years. Georgia stared at the image in the mirror, just a little dismayed. She was older than he was!

Makes no difference to me. I wonder how Mike will feel about that.

Mike arrived at precisely seven o'clock. They drove several miles outside of town to Catfish Heaven, a popular restaurant located on a small hill just a hundred feet from Pine Tree Lake. The dining room featured a glass wall offering a spectacular view of the blue water with tiny ripples pushed along slowly by a gentle breeze. On a Wednesday night, the number of diners was small, and Georgia and Mike chose an isolated table with a red checkered tablecloth, next to the window.

By eight-thirty, they had finished their meal—she had lamb chops while Mike had opted for a sirloin steak—and had just ordered dessert when Mike reached over and covered Georgia's hand with his.

"Would you look at that sunset? I haven't seen such a beautiful one in ages."

Georgia looked out over the lake. The sun was settling down among the pine trees on the far side of the lake, creating a shimmering, golden path across the water and ending at a narrow, sandy beach just down a grassy slope from the restaurant.

"It is beautiful," she said. "Peaceful. Serene." She turned her hand over to take Mike's hand in hers.

As if on cue, the waiter arrived and placed a single dish in the middle of the table. A generous serving of warm apple cobbler, steaming ever so slightly under a slab of vanilla ice cream, filled the air with the pungent scent of cinnamon.

"A delicious end of the meal to accompany the delightful end of the day," the waiter said, putting down a pair of spoons. "Enjoy."

"Shall we?" said Georgia as she picked up a spoon.

Mike grabbed the other spoon and with a devilish grin said, "Reminds me of my favorite grace at meal time when I was a kid."

"Which was?"

"*In the name of the Father, the Son, and the Holy Ghost. The one who eats the fastest, gets the most.*"

Georgia laughed. "I'm sure God is happy to be remembered. Of course, now we say Holy Spirit, which unfortunately, ruins the rhyme."

Mike closed his eyes and crinkled his face. Then, his eyes opened, he grinned again and said, "In the name of the Father, the Son, and the Holy Spirit. Thanks for the food, and putting me near it."

"A poet, no less. Well, you work on the next verse and I'll work on this dessert." Georgia picked up her spoon and scooped out a big bite of pie and ice cream.

Nearly an hour passed before Mike and Georgia strolled outside to admire the moonlight that now highlighted the lake. They had talked over dessert and beyond, on music and sports, from the good points of their professions to what they thought would make a great vacation. She was surprised to find Mike liked classical music. He was surprised to learn Georgia was a basketball fanatic. Both had vacationed in Hawaii and loved it.

For Georgia, it marked the first time since Leo departed for Iraq that she had talked about such things. For the past three years, her conversations had centered on teaching and church activities. And while both of those were close to her heart, she found it exciting to be having a leisurely visit about such diverse and pleasant topics. It didn't hurt that it took place with a very attractive man. *And sexy.* She took a short breath and looked to the side, a tiny smile reflecting her feelings. She realized she had not applied that description to any man since Leo.

They stood on the grassy slope leading down to the lake, Georgia looking at the moonlight dancing on the water, Mike looking at Georgia. He startled her when he ran a fingertip across her cheek, lingering on her small dimple.

"Oh, don't concentrate on the imperfections of my face," she said as she took his hand in hers, moved it away, but held on.

He slipped his other arm around her waist. "Imperfection? It's cute. It's charming. And I'm barely able to resist kissing it."

"Thank you, but I think of it as a flaw. Now, if I had a matching one on the left cheek, maybe..."

"Georgia, you must know how beautiful you are, and that dimple just makes you all the more attractive. I think I'm smitten by you."

She started to object, but he turned her to him, and gently pressed his lips against hers.

Georgia's eyes opened wide, then slowly closed as her breathing accelerated. She found herself confused and uncertain, but she did not break away. Finally, Mike released her and for several moments he just studied her.

He sucked in air. "Let me rephrase that. I am definitely smitten by you, my Georgia peach."

He took her hand and they walked slowly back toward the car.

They made the trip home mostly in silence. Georgia's mind raced as fast as her pulse. She had not kissed a man since Leo had left for Iraq. She had not kissed a man other than Leo in—she counted back—thirteen years. Mike stirred emotions she hadn't felt in a long time. And, it had been nice. Better than nice. Exciting.

Her thoughts reverted to Leo. He had been the love of her life. He was kind and gentle, strong and dependable. Their marriage had been ideal. At least until he went to Iraq. Those last two years had been torture, always worrying, frightened at every telephone call or knock on the door. And then, the fear had become a reality. For a while she didn't believe she could go on. Later, she felt resolved to a life of misery. She dragged herself to work, never smiled, and sometimes spent hours watching the weather channel. Some days, meals consisted of popcorn. And when she picked up the newspaper, she turned to the obituaries.

But she discovered that time did have a healing power and eventually she found pleasure in working at the church, helping others with whatever problems they had. Leo was a fantastic part of her history, and she had not forgotten him. But he was a memory now.

She had been frightened—only now did she admit it—when Mike had first asked her out. She felt as if she had never dated before, had no idea how to act, and was positive she did not want a relationship with a man. But these evenings with Mike had been pleasant. Tonight, standing by the lake, held tightly in a man's arms, parts of her remembered the joy of life.

Was she being foolish? Was this a school girl's reaction? Her mind couldn't judge. She prided herself on being able to look at the facts, quickly understand the pros and cons of each action, and make an intelligent, logical decision. Tonight, she didn't know what to think. She had no idea what the good and bad points might be. The only fact she could bring to mind was that she had enjoyed the moment.

Georgia opened her eyes to realize that, not only was the car in her driveway, but Mike had opened her door and was holding out his hand to help her out. She stammered a thank you and silently, they walked to her door.

She fished the keys out of her purse and unlocked the door. Mike took her in his arms and kissed her. This time, she was not surprised. She found herself leaning into him, becoming an active participant, enjoying the sensations racing through her body.

When they broke apart, she was breathing heavily. She looked into his eyes and said, "Wow."

"Wow is right." He brushed his lips across her cheek and wrapped her in a tight embrace. He whispered in her ear, "Are you going to invite me in?"

She wanted to do just that. Without moving away, she murmured, "No."

Mike leaned back to study her, but he did not take his hands off her. "No? Why not? It really was a wow moment." His eyes glistened.

Georgia pulled away. "Yes it was. And that's exactly why I'm not inviting you in. I'm afraid my emotions are a little out of control right now. I think I need a little breathing room."

His expression turned serious. "I won't take advantage of you."

"You wouldn't have to. No, my emotional system has had all it can take tonight." She gave him a little peck on his cheek. "You have to understand, this is all very new for me."

"Now, I know that's not true."

"Yes. It is. I'm a completely different person than I was—well, let's just say many, many years ago."

"Okay. When can we talk again?" His grin returned. "Notice, I said *talk*. Are you free tomorrow?"

"Call me in the morning. If my common sense is in working order, maybe we could have dinner, or get an ice cream sundae, or something. Right now, I'm not able to make decisions."

She stepped inside and closed the screen door between them. "Mike, I had a wonderful time tonight."

She watched as he walked to his car, got in and left.

She closed the door, looked upward, and whispered. "Thank you."

For some time, Georgia sat in front of her mirror, slowly running a brush through her hair. It took a while before she was able to identify the odd feeling deep inside her.

Guilt.

In slow motion, the realization came into focus. She felt guilty, as if she were cheating on Leo. For many minutes, she stared at her reflection, trying to make sense out of the different emotions vying for control.

She put the brush down and turned to study the picture on the bureau.

"No one can ever take your place, Leo. But you're gone and we will be together again in heaven, probably many years from now. Tonight, someone reminded me of the joy I first learned from you, the electrifying ecstasy that can exist between a man and a woman. You taught me that. And I had forgotten. And I know, as surely as I know you loved me, that you would want me to experience that again."

~ Chapter Twenty-Two ~

Father Frank picked up his Bible and opened it to the bookmark he had placed there last night. *I really should read an hour and a half tonight*, he thought. He looked at the clock. *Well, maybe just my usual.*

But the thought of the church burning reminded him that Detective Mike Oakley had urged him to leave lights on outside the church buildings. He had intended to turn them on at nine, but after his talk with Andy, he had forgotten to do it.

He put the Bible down. "Be back in a minute," he said to the black, leather-bound book his mother had given him when he entered the seminary.

He left the rectory and walked across the yard and the parking lot to the church. *That's odd.* The moon had not quite set, and its waning glow highlighted splinters on the door, around the lock. He hadn't noticed those before. He ran a finger over the area. The edges were sharp, probably new. Now, more carefully, he put his hand on the door handle and gently pulled. It moved. Had he forgotten to lock it? Possibly. Just like he might have failed to notice the splinters before.

He dropped the key into his pocket, eased the door open and peered inside. He could see little in the dim light thrown out by two votive candles that had not yet burned out. He avoided looking at the candles, trying to get his eyes accustomed to the darkness. Then, he slipped in through the half-open door.

This is silly. Getting spooked because you left the door unlocked.

He turned his head and started to reach for the light switch. Just beyond the switch, a small alcove led to the doors for the restrooms. As his eyes adjusted to the darkness, he examined the corner of the wall where it turned. At the very bottom it seemed to jut out, forming a bump that looked remarkably like a foot. Not a likely thing to see in the church at night. He thought of the splinters around the lock, and the open door. He'd feel silly when it turned out to be a song book dropped on the floor. He'd done silly things before.

Now, he looked at the votive candle, trying to get his eyes prepared for more light. He flipped on the switch and kept his focus on the alcove. At the speed of light, this area of the church became visible, including what was now clearly a dirty tennis shoe protruding out from the alcove. It did not move. Carefully, Father Frank inspected the area. He did not see any gas or diesel can. He didn't smell any fuel that might be used to accelerate a fire. What he did see was the small box that had been ripped from the wall, the box where people dropped in coins or bills designated for the poor people in the area.

"I'm afraid the Poor Box is hardly worth robbing," Father Frank said. "I emptied it only a few days ago. I imagine you didn't get five dollars."

For a few seconds, the foot didn't move. Then, suddenly, B.D. jumped out of the alcove, a knife held firmly in front of him.

"You're right. Cheap people of your church gave a measly three dollars and seventy cents. Now, git out of my way."

He wiggled the knife as a warning, like a rattlesnake signaling its presence. Both gave the same message: Don't mess with me. I'm dangerous.

"You was lucky last time. Tricked me. I'm ready for you tonight. Mess with me and I cut you. Cut you bad." His eyes jerked around, as if looking for someone else to appear.

Father Frank remained calm, although he knew a cornered man with a knife could be very dangerous.

"B.D., stealing is a sin. Stealing from the poor is particularly bad. Now, put the money down and you can leave."

The boy let out a scornful laugh. "I'll leave, all right. And I'll take the money with me."

"If you need money for food, you can come to church and ask, and we'll be happy to help you. But stealing is not the way to get it. And we don't give money for drugs."

"I ain't gotta ask. I take what I want. Now get outta my way."

He edged toward the door. Father Frank moved back a step, leaving a passage wide enough for B.D. to go by and out the door. As B.D. came opposite the priest, the teenager swiped out with the knife, directly at Father Frank's chest.

The priest leaned back and at the same time swung out one of his legs. He caught B.D. just behind the knees and knocked the boy off his feet. B.D. grabbed at the wall but that hand still held the money and by the time he turned loose of the change, he was too far down to stop his fall. He hit the floor and the knife skittered away across the vinyl tile, coming to rest against the foot of the holy water font.

Father Frank stepped over and put his hand on B.D.'s back, holding him down. "I'll say it again. If you need help, the church will gladly give it to you. But stealing is a sin and we cannot allow that."

Father Frank replaced the hand on B.D.'s back with his foot, then reached over and retrieved the knife. "I'm going to keep this knife. For my safety and yours. One of us might get hurt if you keep swinging it around. Now, you can get up, leave quietly and agree to come in for counseling, and I won't call the police. But if I have to fight you, I will definitely call the police. What's it going to be?"

"If I fight, you ain't gonna be able to call no police." B.D.'s words were threatening but the tone was hollow bravado.

"That's your decision. I'm going to let you up. I suggest you walk out, go home, and ask God to help you straighten up your life. And come back in the daytime and we can talk about your problems."

Father Frank moved his foot off the boy's back and stepped away, allowing ample room for B.D. to exit. He got to his feet, turned toward the priest and spat in his direction.

"Next time, maybe I just bring diesel and matches." He turned and, muttering so his curses were not distinguishable, left.

Father Frank let out a long breath. Since when did disarming people fall under priestly duties? He walked to the door and looked out. B.D. was running full speed away from the church. In less than thirty seconds, he was lost in the darkness.

The priest gathered up the money scattered on the floor and dropped it back in the box. He would need to mount it back on the wall tomorrow. He turned on the outside lights he deemed sufficient to illuminate the church buildings. The jammed lock worked—sort of. It needed to be replaced. Add lock installer to the list of his priestly duties.

~ CHAPTER TWENTY-THREE ~

The clock hand clicked over to nine just as the telephone rang. Georgia put down her coffee and answered it on the third ring.

"Hi, it's your friendly policeman calling to check on you. I hope you had a good night's sleep."

Georgia's mouth curved into a smile. "Yes, I did, and thank you for calling."

"Have you decided to take another turn at long, revealing conversations?"

Georgia twisted the phone cord around her hand. She hadn't expected Mike to call this early, and truth be known, she had not figured out what to do.

A part of her wanted to say, *Come on over and we'll talk until lunch.* But a small voice said, *Not so fast. Are you really able to evaluate this relationship?*

She knew the answer to that. No, she couldn't. Still, did she have to know the end to make a start? She just had to watch her step along the way.

"Ah, the POPsters have a rehearsal tonight and I should be there. How about tomorrow night? I'll cook something and we can listen to some good music."

"That's a long time off. Guess I'll just have to tough it out."

"You're tough enough."

Georgia replaced the phone in its cradle. He *was* strong. And yet, he seemed so gentle when he talked to her. Sensitive. Caring. Was that all an act? For her benefit? He was a detective, after all. He had to be pretty calloused to stay in that kind of a job. It wasn't a place for the weak of spirit, or the thin-skinned.

And yet, they had talked for many hours already in their short—she had trouble saying it—relationship. Still, that's what came to mind. It sounded more permanent than she was willing to admit. Those hours had told her a considerable amount about him.

And I'm sure he's learned a lot about me. I even talked about Leo at length. Probably shouldn't have. But it is a part of me. Leo helped define who I am. No use trying to hide that. If he can't deal with that, this—there's the R-word again—this relationship surely won't go anywhere.

Father Frank had bought and installed a new lock on the church door, and replaced one of the light bulbs that burned out during the night. He had almost forgotten the Poor Box, until Ms. Zimmerman pointed it out to him after morning Mass. He thanked her, not mentioning that he had seen it last night. He assessed the damage, determined he had the materials to repair and reinstall it, and set about fixing it.

Forty minutes later, he stepped back and surveyed his work.

"Not as good as new. But it will serve its purpose. Actually, it doesn't look bad at all."

He knelt down in the last pew and said a prayer that the problems plaguing Pine Tree would stop, with no more churches lost. He asked God to watch over the youth, protect them from the many temptations surrounding them. He asked God to keep Tim safe and return him to his family. And lastly, he asked God to show him how he might better serve the people of Prince of Peace.

He made it down to the town basketball courts and watched the eleven o'clock game. The boys sweated under the intense sun, calling time out to grab drinks of water, and wipe their faces on the tails of their jerseys. He had to smile, thinking of all the summer days he'd done the same thing. It might be too hot to mow the lawn but it was never too hot to play ball.

From a distance, the mournful sound of a siren floated through the park. Father Frank stiffened and caught his breath.

Surely it wouldn't be a church fire in the middle of the day. All the others had been late at night. The frightful sound was coming closer now. Father Frank looked around, trying to focus on the direction of the noise. And then he saw it. An ambulance streaked across an intersection, aimed toward the hospital. Father Frank let out his breath.

Please, God, watch over the patient in the ambulance. And thank you that it's not another church.

Across the park, he saw Earl speaking with some teenagers. They didn't play in Father Frank's basketball league, but they were kids. Earl didn't have any business talking to them. *At least, I hope he doesn't have any business with them.* The priest got up and started over, but before he had covered fifty feet, Earl left.

"Hi, guys," Father Frank said. "What did that man want?"

The boys looked uncomfortable, one studying the ground, another checking his shoes, and a boy with silver studs in both ears mumbled something completely unintelligible to Father Frank.

"He's bad news, guys. He will only get you into trouble, or worse. Please, don't let him get you into something you can't get out of." He looked at each of the group. No reaction.

"Listen, if you ever need to talk, have a problem you want help with, anything at all, come see me. I'm at Prince of Peace, over on Vine Street. You don't have to go to church there to come and talk. And I won't betray your confidence. Okay?"

Again, he looked at each one, hoping for a nod of the head, or some indication that he was getting through to them. None responded. He continued to look from one to another.

Finally, the kid with the ear studs said, "Yeah. Got it. Vine Street."

Father Frank nodded and smiled, then turned and went back to the basketball game, wondering if he had wasted his time.

No. If even one stays away from Earl, I didn't waste my time.

Father Frank was in the middle of lunch when the phone rang.

"We've got a man down here that fits your description. Can you come down and take a look?"

"And hello to you too, Mike," said Father Frank.

"Things are a bit hectic right now. Can you come?" asked the detective.

"Twenty minutes."

"Harley Fewks," said Mike.

Father Frank stood looking through a window into an interrogation room. The paper-cross burning man sat slouched in a chair not nearly big enough for him. Father Frank thought he looked more irritated than worried. His lips curled into a snarl. His jeans had grease on both legs, and his short-sleeved tee, with one sleeve missing, also sported dark stains. The black tennis shoes probably started out white. A paper cup of coffee sat on the desk in front of him. He reached out, picked it up and drank some, spilling a little on the table. He looked at the brown liquid on the table and smirked.

"Look at his hand," said Father Frank. "Looks like he's burned his thumb and forefinger."

"Yeah. Said he did it grilling hamburgers," said Mike. "Somehow, he doesn't look like the outdoor barbeque type to me."

Father Frank laughed. "Not to me either. But when he burned that paper cross, the fire did get pretty close to his hand."

"Which hand was holding the cross?"

Father Frank closed his eyes and tried to picture the scene. "I'm pretty sure he held the paper with his left hand and struck the match with his right."

"So, that burn probably didn't come from the Corral," said Mike.

For a minute, they stood and watched the large, angry man. "What has he said?" asked Father Frank.

"Surprise, surprise. He denied knowing anything about the church fires. Said he could come up with an alibi for any time we wanted."

"Convenient."

"I thought so. Anyway, we ran some tests, just in case there was any diesel residue on his hands. Of course, he'd have just said he pumped diesel for a friend, and I'm sure he could find a friend to back that up. So basically, we've got nothing on him, unless you want to put in a formal complaint on the car incident. We can call that reckless endangerment or something, and hold him for a day or so."

Father Frank shook his head. "No. No harm done. I can take his yelling and taunting. But I certainly wouldn't take him off the suspect list."

Mike reached up to scratch his ear. "He asked us what the big deal was. Just some old buildings. Town was better off without those shacks. I mentioned to him that a person was dead, to which he said. 'Accident. Guy shouldn't a been there.'"

Once more, the priest shook his head, this time in wonderment. "I still can't get over his saying maybe those churches needed to be burned."

"And yours might be next?"

"That certainly got my attention. By the way, I ran into B.D. yesterday, angry as usual. He made a veiled threat against Prince of Peace."

"B.D. Rake? We'll pull him in and talk to him."

Father Frank waved that aside. "I don't think he meant it. Just wanted to rattle my cage." He paused briefly. "Oh, I did leave the lights on last night."

"Good. Keep 'em burning." A look of chagrin crossed the detective's face. "Oops, I guess that's not a good thing to say."

"Not right now. I'll keep them *turned on*," said Father Frank.

"Okay. Oh— " Mike snapped his fingers. "Forgot to tell you. Not that we didn't already know, but the M.E. confirmed that Josephson was killed by blunt force trauma. Dead before smoke or fire got to him."

"So, definitely murder."

"Yeah. 'Course it was anyway. Somebody dies in a fire set by an arsonist, it's murder. But now, it's premeditated murder."

"And Fewks said Josephson shouldn't have been there." Father Frank frowned and tilted his head to the side. "What did he mean by that? Fewks didn't expect anybody to be there? Josephson had no business being in the church? What?"

"Beats me. You can imagine ol' Harley isn't too forthcoming. I won't repeat what he said. What he suggested was physically impossible, anyway." Mike shook his head in disgust. "Guess we have to cut him loose. Want to leave first?"

"I don't want to look like I'm afraid of that tub of lard," said the priest. "Pardon me for that uncharitable statement. But it might be less of a problem for you if I'm not here. If he sees me, he might get wild again."

"Probably right. I'll walk you out."

The two headed for the front of the police station.

"That Georgia is quite a woman," said Mike.

"That she is," replied Father Frank. "She spends a lot of time helping others. Most of our projects would never happen without her. But she religiously makes sure someone else gets all the credit. A true Christian."

"Put in a good word for me."

"She tells me you're a Catholic. How come you never come to Mass?"

They had reached the front door. "Long story."

"I've got time."

"I don't. Got to go take care of Harley," said Mike, turning to go.

"Some other time, Mike. It *is* important. Whatever the problem, I'm sure we can work it out."

Mike was heading back down the hall. Over his shoulder he said, "Maybe later."

~ CHAPTER TWENTY-FOUR ~

Father Frank headed over to see how the POPsters were progressing during rehearsal. Half way there, a boy that Father Frank had seen at the park that afternoon, the one with studs in both ears, intercepted him. Father Frank was genuinely surprised.

"Hi. What's on your mind?"

"Ah, just thought I'd tell you what Earl said." His focus shifted between the priest and the ground.

"I'd appreciate that."

"He asked if we knowed where a person could score? Did we know who the big dog was, who ran the meth around here? He really pushed on the meth."

"What'd you tell him?"

"Nothin'. One of the guys said he thought you could get stuff at The Corral. Or maybe over on Grove Street." He shifted his weight from one foot to the other.

Father Frank studied the boy for a minute. "Did he try to sell you anything? Or offer to give you anything?"

"No. Couple of the guys know more'n they was saying." He held up his hand. "Not me. But I seen a couple of 'em with some weed the other day."

"Listen, I really appreciate you talking with me." The priest glanced at the ball cap the boy was wearing. "Your cap looks nice. But what do you have all around the edge of the bill?"

"Thumb tacks." His tone said that was obvious.

"Okay. Why thumb tacks?"

"The different colors look cool." He touched the under-side of the bill. "And they stick through on the bottom, so nobody can, you know, grab it off my head."

Father Frank chuckled, and then, turned serious. "If you ever need any help, please come and see me."

"Yeah. Well, maybe."

The kid turned and slouched off, the bottoms of his baggy pants dragging on the ground.

Inside the church hall, Father Frank listened to the POPsters.

"Amazing progress they're making," he said to Phyllis and Georgia.

"Yes." Phyllis almost gushed. "Roger is doing fantastically well. And he loves it. When we get home after a practice, he just beams. It's really revved up his life. And the kids. They even ask if they can have more practices."

The priest grinned. He remembered thinking Roger was sort of stodgy. Not anymore. He had the energy of a teenager, which was good since he was working with twenty-eight of them. Father Frank checked the group, counted. No, now there were thirty-three.

"I understand next month's concert is now a benefit for the burned churches."

"Yes. Georgia, tell him what we're planning."

"It's your chorus. You tell him. I just help out," Georgia said.

Phyllis looked a little embarrassed but her enthusiasm overcame that. "Well, we're going for two concerts. We've raised the prices and we're getting sponsors. I got the newspaper today. They've pledged five hundred dollars, *and* they're giving us free advertising. I think we can raise twelve thousand." She beamed at the priest.

"That's great, Phyllis. And when is this event?" Father Frank asked.

"Three weeks from next Friday—the last Friday before football season starts." Phyllis' eyes sparkled and her entire face glowed. Her hands fidgeted. "Once the season starts, we'd have to fight football for—for everything. Roger says they'll be ready."

"It's on the master church calendar," said Georgia. "You've been too busy to look, I take it."

Father Frank smiled. "A little busy. I think all three of you are to be praised and thanked. This is a great thing for the kids. And the lesson you're teaching, to help those in need, is priceless."

"It was the kid's idea," said Georgia. "They wanted to help. Phyllis and I pointed them in the right direction."

He patted Georgia on the shoulder but looked at Phyllis. "Keep up the good work, Phyllis. And tell Roger how impressed I am."

The insistent buzzing of the doorbell disrupted Father Frank's concentration.

Go away, he thought.

But then, he remembered the subject of the sermon he was working on: "You *Are* Your Brother's Keeper."

He could not ignore the call for his attention. Who would be ringing his bell after midnight? Whoever it was rang the bell again, this time leaning on it. Father Frank trudged into the living room and opened the door.

Earl stood glaring at him.

~ Chapter Twenty-Five ~

Earl had a four-day growth of black stubble. His hair looked dirty. The beige knit shirt showed sweat stains under both arms. And his eyes were tired and angry.

The priest was too weary to back off, or even say anything to his nemesis.

In his usual gruff voice, Earl said, "Got B.D. here."

Father Frank stuck his head out the door. B.D. leaned against the house, head on his chest, eyes closed, breathing erratically. At that moment, a shudder went through him and Earl had to put his hand on the boy's shoulder to keep him from falling.

"He's in bad shape. OD'd on some junk. Get him to the emergency room. Now." As usual, Earl's tone and delivery brooked no argument.

Father Frank looked from Earl to B.D. and back to Earl. "What have you done to him? What did you give him?" The priest's adrenaline level shot up, along with his blood pressure.

"I haven't done anything to him. He did it to himself. Are you going to get him some help, or let him die right here on your porch?"

"Why didn't you take him there, instead of here?"

"We don't have time to argue. Get your keys and get moving." The volume of Earl's voice dropped, the cadence slowed. This was not a request. "I'm putting him in your car. Get your keys."

With that, he turned, put B.D.'s arm over his shoulder and practically carried him off the porch and across the drive to Father Frank's car. He leaned the boy on the front fender of the

Taurus, readjusting him twice to keep him from sliding off the car. Earl opened the front passenger side door. When he went back to B.D., the boy's legs buckled and his arms fell limp at his sides. Earl caught him before he fell, picked him up, and put him in the car.

When Earl came back to the house, Father Frank was still standing in the door, hands on hips, watching with a wrinkled forehead.

"Get your keys." The power in Earl's voice rose sharply. "I swear he's going to die in your car if you don't get moving."

Father Frank straightened up and looked Earl directly in the eyes. "I don't know what you're doing here. You can take that boy to the hospital as easily as I can. Why are you afraid to do that?"

Earl glared at the priest, his eyes burning coals, his mouth as angry as a shark's. The look would have withered most people, but Father Frank did not move.

He met Earl's fierce look and said, "I'm not moving until I get some answers."

Father Frank forced himself to sound resolute, but knew if he didn't get an answer in the next minute, he'd rush B.D. to the hospital.

"Do what you want. He's in your car. Take him to the hospital or take him to the morgue. I'm gone." With that, the big, burly man turned and walked away.

B.D.'s breathing was even rougher now, ragged, raspy, erratic. His eyes remained closed and he was crumpled against the door like a rag doll.

"Hold on, B.D. We'll be at the hospital in five minutes."

As he started the car, the priest prayed.

Dear God, take pity on this misguided soul, help him regain his health, and find his way back to You. Please, Lord. Forgive B.D. his wrongs. And if he cannot recover, please welcome him into Your house.

Now, a different set of questions rushed into his mind from all sides, like a dozen children wanting to be answered at the same time. What had B.D. taken? Or been given? What was Earl doing with B.D.? Had he given B.D. drugs? Is that why he wouldn't take him to the hospital? And why did he bring the boy to Prince of Peace?

As Father Frank pulled up to the emergency door, a frightening fact popped up in his mind. Drug use in Pine Tree was no longer remote, no longer a problem "over there."

Earl had dropped it into Father Frank's lap.

~ Chapter Twenty-Six ~

Between meeting with the Faith Formation teachers and the fledging women's guild, and then having two private consultations, it was after noon before Father Frank got back to the hospital to check on B.D. The priest's spirits fell when he received the news. B.D. was in a coma. He had indeed overdosed on drugs, a particularly strong strain that attacked the nerves. Too much and it shut down some of the body's systems. The doctor explained the details, but Father Frank was too dazed to follow.

"Because of his age, he has a chance of making it," the doctor continued. "But from what we can tell, his system has been weakened by other drug use, or alcohol abuse, probably over a period of months. Right now, we can't say whether he'll survive or not."

"When will you know—?"

"It will be at least a day or two, maybe more. Sorry to have to tell you that."

Guilt reared up in Father Frank's mind. "Doctor, would it have made any difference if he had been brought in ten minutes earlier? Before he blacked out completely?"

The doctor looked down, considered that for a few moments, then looked back up at the priest. "Probably not. An hour earlier, I'd say probably yes. Ten, fifteen minutes? No. Why?"

Father Frank swallowed. "I didn't act as quickly as I might. He could have been brought here five minutes faster." He thought of Earl taking B.D. to Prince of Peace and not the hospital. "Maybe ten minutes."

"My guess is he was not your responsibility. You brought him here and gave him a chance, one he didn't give himself."

The doctor fixed Father Frank with a stern look and gave an order as he might issue to a nurse. "Do *not* feel bad you didn't react faster. This is not your fault. You made the situation better, not worse. Ten minutes wouldn't change the outcome."

All in all, the report left Father Frank depressed. The doctor said B.D.'s system was already weakened before this overdose. He said he had a chance, but he didn't say a *good* chance. The doctor wouldn't even say B.D. would probably survive.

B.D. was a young kid who should have a life ahead of him. Drugs had ensnared him and now he was fighting to have a life at all.

Father Frank stopped in the hospital chapel and knelt to pray for B.D., to ask God to give him another chance. He thought of his childhood friend.

Don't let B.D. lose to drugs, like Rick did.

Father Frank tried to take the doctor's words to heart but guilt haunted his thoughts, like some grotesque gargoyle, threatening to devour his spirit.

You should have moved faster. You should have moved faster. You should have saved Rick.

On the drive home, Father Frank detoured by the service station to put fuel in the Taurus. He finished pumping the gas and was waiting for the machine to spit out the credit card slip when Harley Fewks skidded into the station. He got out of his truck, slammed the door and grabbed the diesel hose, ready to fill a five gallon can he held in his beefy hand. That's when his gaze settled on Father Frank.

"Well, look who's here. The sissy priest."

~ Chapter Twenty-Seven ~

Fewks stomped over to position himself within inches of Father Frank. "I oughta pound your tattle *tail* into the pavement."

Father Frank took a deep breath, determined to stay calm. "I'm sorry you feel that way."

"Sorry? You caused it. Police drug me down there again. Then, like that ain't enough, one of 'em come to my place. I don't like police comin' to my place. You know why he come?"

He waited only a moment before answering his own question, spitting out the words.

"'Cause *you* sicced him on me."

As much as Father Frank wanted to punch the windbag, he knew that was hardly the priestly thing to do.

"Look, Harley. Several churches have been burned. It wasn't a good time to do what you did. Anyone would consider it inflammatory."

"Inflammatory," Fewks said with as much disdain as possible. "Maybe I oughta inflammatory you." He sneered. "Better yet, your church."

Father Frank stuffed his hands in his pockets and gritted his teeth in a battle to keep from smacking Harley in the face. And he was losing that fight. Any minute and he would forget he was a priest and show Harley that speed and conditioning trumped fat and out of shape.

The only thing to do was remove himself from temptation. In his mind, he recited, "Blessed are the peacemakers, for they shall be called the children of God. Blessed are they that suffer persecution for justice's sake, for theirs is the kingdom of heaven."

The priest turned and started to walk away.

Harley Fewks was not ready to quit. He grabbed Father Frank's shoulder and spun him around.

"We ain't through yet, sissy priest."

By now, several people were looking on, watching the altercation. Father Frank recognized two boys from the basketball league.

Another kid with studs in both ears and wearing a ball cap with thumb tacks pushed through the visor, yelled, "Punch his lights out, Father."

Father Frank looked over at the boy. "Fighting isn't the way to settle disagreements."

The priest believed that, although at this moment, his heart was not in the statement.

"Yeah," mocked Fewks. "When you ain't really a man, you don't wanna fight like a man."

Forgive me, Lord, the priest prayed.

He faced Harley. "I don't want to fight you, Harley."

Fewks threw his head back and roared. "Guess not, sissy priest."

"How about we settle this by arm wrestling? You win, and I'll apologize in front of all these people. And you'll look good. If I win, you just back off, quit yelling in my face. Are you willing to risk that—against a sissy priest?"

Harley slapped his leg and laughed. "I'll put you down so fast and hard, you'll think your arm broke."

The two men positioned themselves at the back corner of the Taurus, Harley Fewks behind the back bumper, Father Frank at the back right fender. The crowd watching had grown to seven people. The boy who had yelled before, stepped forward.

"I'll referee. Take your positions. Don't start pushing till I say go."

"Don't need you," Harley growled. He moved his feet, trying to get his ample stomach just right.

"Yeah, you do. Don't want no cheatin' goin' on here. Don't want the priest pulling a fast one on you," the boy in the ball cap said.

Father Frank settled his arm on the back of the trunk. He positioned and repositioned his feet, making sure he had good balance. Harley did the same thing. Father Frank's muscular arm looked small against Harley's thick arm which was decorated with half a dozen tattoos. Then, Harley's beefy hand grabbed Father Frank's and immediately began trying to push it down.

A mix of feelings bobbed around in Father Frank's head. Whoever won the arm wrestle, Father Frank would come out ahead. He could apologize to Harley, particularly if that ended the verbal attacks. On the other hand, Father Frank's competitive spirit wanted to come out on top. And he hated to see the angry man win.

"Okay," the boy said. "I'm gonna say one, two, three, then go. Don't start 'fore I say go, or you gets disqualified."

He looked at Father Frank. "You ready?"

The priest nodded.

The boy turned to Harley. "Ready?"

Fewks said, "Yeah. Let's get it on."

The boy counted slowly. "One, two, three. Go."

Fewks immediately shoved his hand over and brought the priest's hand halfway down to the trunk lid.

"This'll be quick."

But at that point, Father Frank stiffened and stopped the movement. Slowly, Father Frank began to force his hand back up to vertical.

He may be fat and out of shape, the priest thought, *but he does have a strong arm.*

Father Frank forced Harley's hand over, nearly halfway down. But he could get it no lower. Now, Father Frank was beginning to feel the strain. Beads of sweat formed on his forehead. For a moment, he thought he was going to lose. He glanced up. Sweat covered Harley's face. Father Frank clamped his jaw shut as his breathing became more labored. He hated to lose. And he really didn't want to lose to Harley Fewks.

I don't have to force his hand down just yet. Wear him down. The coach always said conditioning will pay off.

The minutes crept by. Father Frank was aware of another car driving up for gas, but instead of operating the pump, the driver came over to watch. While there had been talk among the crowd when the contest started, the priest realized it was very quiet now. The only noise was an occasional grunt from Harley.

Father Frank closed his eyes. *Dear Lord, I know I'm letting pride take control of me. But this man has ridiculed Your churches. Please forgive me, if pride is clouding my mind.*

Their heads were only inches apart. With no demands on his brain, Father Frank's senses took notice of everything around him. The burning in his arm. The faded paint on the trunk of his car. The silence of the people watching. And the smell of smoke. And diesel. He cut his eyes up to look at Harley.

Maybe the diesel smell is coming from the pump behind me.

But the smell of smoke was coming from Harley. Father Frank's brain posed a question. Is that smoke from The Corral? Or New Beginnings Baptist Church?

For what seemed like ages to Father Frank, their locked hands had not moved. Harley made periodic attempts, gaining nothing. Father Frank was saving his strength until he felt a weakness in his opponent. He could feel sweat running down their arms but couldn't tell if it was coming from Harley, himself, or both of them.

Once more, Father Frank shifted his focus to look at Harley. His scraggy mustache was soaked and periodically sweat dripped from one end or the other. Suddenly, Harley's elbow came off the trunk lid and he raised his arm above their hands and began to push Father Frank's arm down.

"Elbow down on the car," yelled the referee.

Several others in the crowd yelled.

"Not Fair."

"Play by the rules."

"Get your elbow down."

Harley's elbow sank back to the metal, and his advantage ceased as quickly as it started. Now, Father Frank could feel Harley's arm begin to quiver slightly. Still the priest did not try to pin his opponent.

Another minute passed. Father Frank could hear Harley's breathing starting to come in gasps, and a low rumble came from within. Again, Father Frank glanced up to look at his opponent. He could see sweat streaming down Harley's face, dripping from his mustache, and became more aware of the strong body odor radiating from Harley.

The crowd had grown to ten, as another man walked up. "What's going on? Having an arm-wrestling contest?"

"Shhh," came from several of the people.

Father Frank, head down, sweat dripping off the end of his nose, rolled his eyes up for another look at Fewks. The big man's head was shaking ever so slightly, like a leaf in a gentle breeze. One of the tattoos on his right arm was a heart. The muscles in his arm were quivering, giving the impression that the tattooed heart was beating.

Now is the time.

Slowly, Father Frank increased the pressure. Gradually, the beefy arm began to move. Father Frank could feel Fewks' strain, his arm and head shaking more noticeably, the low grunt becoming louder. The downward movement stopped. For thirty seconds, the arms did not move.

Father Frank watched the drops of salty water falling on the trunk lid until a small pool encircled both elbows. His arm ached, burned like a branding iron rested on it. The pain reminded him of the fire that had taken three of God's churches in less than two weeks. That image increased his determination. He could feel Harley's resistance fading. Father Frank took a deep breath and held it as he strained to make a final push, and with a jerk, he slammed Harley Fewks' arm down on the trunk lid.

The crowd let out a spontaneous cheer.

Both men straightened up, breathing hard, and wiped the sweat out of their eyes, off their foreheads.

The self-declared referee turned to the crowd and confirmed, "Father Frank is the winner!"

The crowd murmured its agreement, and applause erupted.

With hate in his eyes, Harley Fewks glared at his opponent. He leaned in close and hissed, "Won't yell at you no more. But I'll be watchin' you. And your church. Sometimes, accidents happen."

He held the position and sneered at the priest. Then abruptly, the big man straightened up and, rubbing his arm, walked past Father Frank, 'accidentally' colliding with the priest's shoulder and almost knocking him to the ground.

CHAPTER TWENTY-EIGHT

As soon as Father Frank got back to the rectory, he phoned Mike. "I don't want to be an alarmist, but as I was driving back from... back to the church, I stopped at the Shell station. Harley Fewks came in and bought five gallons of diesel. In a container."

"Thanks for observing and reporting." Mike let out an audible breath. "Didn't I tell you to stay out of this? For your information, I've already been in contact with Mister Fewks this morning. The lab came up with diesel on his hands, so I went to talk to him. Turns out, he's got a Kubota 7800 diesel. A pretty small tractor. It probably makes sense to buy fuel five gallons at a pop."

Father Frank thought of Fewks' parting remarks, hesitated a moment, trying to decide how much to tell Mike. What Fewks had said was the result of frustration and anger, not necessarily signifying any intention.

"Well, I just thought I'd mention it."

"Glad you did. I'm not writing old Harley off. But he's got a reason for the diesel. In fact, we've asked all the service stations if anyone made any unusual purchases of diesel—someone they knew had no need for it. No luck there." He paused just a beat.

"Heard you brought one B.D. Rake to emergency last night."

"That's right."

"Report said you found him on your porch."

"Yes."

"Just hanging out on your porch? Maybe wanted to buy a Bible? Or get your take on the Rangers?"

"No. Actually, Earl brought him. Claims he found B.D. in bad shape and brought him over for me to take to the hospital."

"And he didn't have enough gas to make the hospital?"

"I asked him why he brought B.D. to me instead of taking him directly to emergency. He didn't answer. Just said I could take the boy or let him die."

"And you didn't think this was important enough to put in the report?"

Father Frank took a deep breath. Of course Mike was right. "Yes. I should have put that in the report. At the time, I was in a bit of shock myself. Sorry. I apologize for not putting it in."

"So, maybe he caused B.D. to overdose, or maybe Earl gave him some bad stuff. And he didn't want to answer any questions about his involvement."

"That was my guess," said the priest. "He didn't want B.D. to die—for whatever reason. But didn't want to answer questions either."

"We need to talk to Earl." Mike tapped on the phone for a few seconds. "Please don't make my job harder by withholding information." Mike paused only a second. "Anything else you want to add?"

Once more, Father Frank considered mentioning the veiled threat Harley had made just before he left. He decided against it. He was beginning to sound like a crybaby.

"No. Not now."

Father Frank had a late supper, then drove to the hospital to check on B.D. once more. The nurse reported that B.D. had not regained consciousness yet, but he was breathing better and his vital signs had improved. She sounded more optimistic than the doctor had earlier in the day. Father Frank wondered if that simply reflected a more optimistic nurse.

She said no visitors were allowed in but the priest could look in from the door. Father Frank stood for a moment, studying the boy. Even with all the IV's and monitors, B.D. looked more peaceful than the other times Father Frank had seen him.

As before, he stopped in the chapel and asked God to help this young man, both physically and spiritually.

He walked out to the parking lot thinking that if, heaven forbid, there was another church fire now, B.D. had a perfect alibi. He got into his car, started the engine but did not shift into drive. Something was niggling at his brain. He had, perhaps arbitrarily, come up with four suspects, as Monsignor Decker had called them. Earl stood at the top of the list. Father Frank had little doubt that Earl was involved in the Pine Tree drug scene. But why would he bring B.D. to the rectory? A soft spot in his heart—didn't want the kid to die? Or just didn't want to lose a customer? Didn't want to answer any questions at the hospital? Whatever the reason, it did not change Earl's position on the suspect list.

Unfortunately, Father Frank didn't have a clue as to whether any of the four had alibis for any of the fires.

A clue.

What information *did* he have? Not much. And then, he groaned as he snapped his fingers. *Of course.*

Sammie.

Sammie was the key. Sammie had plunged Father Frank into this. And yet, Sammie had given no clues. At least, that's what Father Frank had been thinking.

Wrong.

Sammie had provided two important pieces of information. One, the arsonist had to be a friend, or at least an acquaintance of Sammie's. If he had heard about this on the street, why not say who it was? If he knew the person only slightly, perhaps just met him, why not tell? And the fact that Sammie had known information about more than one fire implied he had a more permanent relationship, or at least connection, with the arsonist.

The second fact—perhaps 'fact' was a little strong—came from his behavior. Either he felt a strong sense of loyalty to the person burning the churches or he feared the person.

Father Frank banged his hand on the steering wheel. Why hadn't he thought of this before?

Of course, Sammie might know all four of Father Frank's suspects. For now, he would forget about B.D. He threatened nobody while he was unconscious in a hospital bed. Father Frank had no trouble believing Sammie might be afraid of Harley Fewks but he had a hard time believing Sammie would be a friend or acquaintance of Harley. The same reasoning applied to Earl. With one exception. Earl connected with the teenagers much more than Harley did. But with Sammie? Father Frank had trouble seeing Sammie with Earl.

Am I being blind? Could Sammie be involved with Earl? Or with Fewks?

And then there's Ward. Father Frank had seen Sammie with Ward, who had identified himself as a friend of Sammie's.

Replaying the scene in his mind, Father Frank remembered how nervous Sammie seemed. He had wound and rewound a string around his thumb. Even as he spoke to Father Frank, he kept glancing back at Ward, as if checking to see Ward's reaction.

Sammie was afraid of Ward.

Father Frank had seen a diesel can in Ward's house. Not conclusive of anything. But it did offer means. Motive remained a puzzle no matter which suspect Father Frank considered. Still, in the third fire, Josephson was murdered. Here again, nothing irrefutable, but perhaps Ward knew Josephson. And Ward stored a great amount of anger. Father Frank sighed. Considering Ward's background, the anger should not come as a surprise.

Of course, Fewks could have known Josephson. Fewks had enough rage to commit murder given the right circumstances. It might be worthwhile to check into Josephson's background. Surely there were still people around who knew him when he was here before. Or during his current stay.

Father Frank knew where Ward lived but didn't know where Fewks lived, although most likely he could find out easily. Perhaps Ward would be home this time of day. Less than a half hour of light remained. Why not just drive by and see if he was at home? Father Frank put the car in gear and headed toward the milk plant.

As he drove, a disturbing fact forced its way into his mind. As much as he hated to admit it, Sammie stood squarely in the middle of things. In fact, of all the people Father Frank tried to link to the fires, only one could he absolutely connect. Sammie. He knew about the fires even before they happened. Could he have set them? Father Frank felt his throat tighten as his mind struggled with the possibility.

If Sammie had set the fires, why come tell it in confession? That was easy; to be absolved. But then—if in fact Sammie caused any of the fires—he went back and burned another church. The priest shook his head. Certainly, some people committed the same sin over and over, addicted as if it were a powerful drug.

Pyromaniacs had an obsessive desire or need to set a fire. He had read that some got a high watching a building burn. The bigger the fire, the bigger the high.

"No." He closed his eyes and tilted his face upward. "I won't believe Sammie burned those churches."

The priest frowned as he opened his eyes.

But was he involved? More accurately, how *was he involved*?

Father Frank passed the milk plant and two minutes later parked in front of Ward's small, neat house. The sun was sinking fast now, and the trees at the back cast long shadows across the yard. Dark shapes undulated, giving the eerie appearance of unearthly waifs dancing in the yard. For an instant, they reminded Father Frank of the dancing flames of the burning churches. A slight shiver ran down his back.

He studied the area carefully. He saw no vehicles, no sign of life. Most likely Ward was not at home but Father Frank walked up and knocked on the door. He thought about the diesel can he had seen in the kitchen two days ago. Probably as simple an explanation as Mike had given him for Harley. As the detective said, this was rural East Texas. Diesel fuel was a staple. Still, there was no evidence of a tractor here. What did he know about Ward? Nothing. Maybe he drove a diesel car.

But the thought nagged at him, and he decided to go take another look, see if the diesel can was still in the kitchen. He checked the road in both directions. No one coming. No Ward Campo making his way home at that precise moment.

As before, all the shades were pulled closed. *Probably helps keep the heat out. Doesn't mean he's hiding anything.* In the back, he went to the door and peered through the key hole. No diesel can in view. He pulled away, then bent to look once more. A small bar of light crossed the floor, about where the fuel can had been before. He had initially thought it was just the fact that the can had been removed. But no.

It was light, sunlight playing on the floor. How did it get in? He started to move back and the light changed. Odd. It was as if he had changed it by moving.

He stepped back to look at the door again. The shade was pulled down as before. Almost. Today, it did not cover the glass completely. A quarter inch gap existed between the bottom of the glass and the bottom of the shade. From a distance, it was inconspicuous. Even at close range, with the room dark, it had escaped Father Frank's notice.

He brought his eyes close to the gap. This view, though still restricted, gave him an opportunity to see much more of the room. It was, as he had guessed, a kitchen. He now could see a stove and a refrigerator.

His eyes opened wide. Lying on the floor in front of the refrigerator was a body.

The body of a boy.

~ CHAPTER TWENTY-NINE ~

Father Frank banged on the door with his fist and yelled. The body jerked, struggling to turn. He managed to move slightly. Now, Father Frank could see the ropes. The boy was tied. Probably gagged, since no sound came from the room. Had somebody robbed Ward, and left him tied up and helpless? With no one else living there, he might not be found for days.

The priest looked around, then ran to the burn barrel. The sun had slipped below the horizon and light was fading fast. He bent low, trying to see but could not find what he needed.

Stepping heel to toe, he began moving in a spiral around and away from the barrel. On the third pass, his foot came down on something thin and hard. He picked up the piece of reinforcing rod and raced back to the door.

He broke the glass and with four quick strokes, cleared the rest of the glass out of the frame. He pulled the shade down an inch and released it, letting it flap up to the top. Careful where he put his hands, he climbed into the kitchen.

He turned the body over. In the last bit of light, Sammie Winters stared up at him, fear dominating his features.

"Heavens, Sammie, what's going on?" Father Frank worked to loosen the end of the grey tape covering Sammie's mouth.

"This is going to hurt, but quick is best." He yanked on the tape and it ripped off. A short cry escaped from the boy.

Once the tape was gone, Sammie said, "He's going to burn Prince of Peace." Father Frank could hear the fear in the boy's whimper. "He's gone there now."

The twilight glow had ended and the tiny kitchen faded into blackness. The priest worked on the ropes, but the knots were tight and his fingers were fat sausages tonight, uncharacteristically clumsy, incapable of loosening the tangle of rope. Untying the knots became impossible as darkness filled the room.

"Sammie, where's the light switch in here?"

"I, uh, I don't remember. Maybe by the door."

"Which door?"

"I..." It came out as a moan. "... don't know."

"That's okay, Sammie. Don't worry. Just give me a few minutes and I'll have you free."

The priest groped around, trying to find the switch. He bumped into the table, sending the salt and pepper shakers clattering to the floor.

"Doesn't seem to be by the door to the living room."

He made his way toward the back door, kicking one of the shakers on his way, and knocking a chair over. He was only a few feet from the door, when he stepped on some of the glass that now littered the floor. His feet shot out from under him and he fell heavily. His hand found more of the glass as he levered himself up.

"Ouch."

"Are you all right, Father?"

"I sliced my hand and it hurts like the devil. But otherwise, I'm okay... I think."

He got up and ran his hand along the wall around the door. "I still can't find the light switch. I guess I'm just going to have to..."

"Over the table," Sammie said, animation coloring his voice now. "The light hangs down over the table. You turn it on over the bulb. You know, a twisty switch on the socket holding the bulb."

Father Frank worked his way back to the middle of the room until he hit the table with his thigh. Carefully, he swung his hand around over the table until he felt the glass bulb. A moment later, light filled the room.

He began opening drawers. On the third one, he found a knife. Carefully, he cut the ropes and freed Sammie's hands, and then his feet.

"Are you okay?" Father Frank asked as he helped Sammie to his feet.

"Yeah. Sore from being tied up." He glanced down at the priest's hand. "Your hand looks terrible."

"Feels terrible, too." He looked around, found a piece of cloth and wrapped it around his bleeding hand. "Let's get out of here."

With his left hand, he grabbed the door and tried to open it. But the skeleton lock didn't respond to the handle and no key was in sight.

"Can you climb out the top?" he asked Sammie.

"Sure. How 'bout you? I mean with your hand and all."

"I'll make it. You said Ward was going to burn Prince of Peace? Tonight?"

Sammie was already climbing through the top half of the door.

"Careful," Father Frank cautioned.

"There's probably some jagged glass still in the edges of the door."

"I'm okay." Sammie hit the back step and stumbled, but kept his footing. "Here, let me help you."

In less than a minute, the two had seat-belted themselves into the Taurus and were driving toward Prince of Peace. Now would be a good time to have a cell phone, Father Frank thought.

"Has Ward burned all three of the churches?"

"Yes." The boy said it so softly, the priest almost missed it.

"Tell me why, Sammie. Why burn churches?"

"I don't know."

"Come on, Sammie. Tell me what you do know."

A soft sniffle came from the passenger side of the seat.

"What is it, Sammie?"

"It's my fault he's going to burn Prince of Peace."

"Your fault. Why is that? How is it your fault?" The priest tried to look at Sammie but he was driving too fast to take his eyes off the road.

"I came over to tell him I wasn't having nothin' else to do with fires. I said he should go talk with you, that you'd help him. That got him mad. Said it was, you know, 'cause the church was feeding me a lot of bull. The church had turned me against him."

Father Frank glanced at Sammie, but said nothing.

"I said that wasn't it. He kinda laughed and said if I didn't care, we'd go burn Prince of Peace. He knew that's where I go."

Sammie looked out the window, turning his head away from the priest. "Ward's been, you know, crazy the last couple of weeks."

When Sammie said nothing else, Father Frank asked, "Why did he tie you up?"

"I said I wasn't gonna watch him burn my church. That's when he knocked me down. Put his knee in my back and tied me up. I started screaming at him, you know, that he couldn't burn my church. And he just laughed and slapped that tape over my mouth."

"And you don't know why he burned the other churches?"

"No. I mean, after the last one, when the guy got killed, I said he had to stop. Somebody got killed in the fire, and he said the guy got what he deserved."

Father Frank looked at the boy. "What did he mean by that? Why did the man deserve to die?"

Sammie shook his head. "I don't know. He didn't tell me."

Father Frank pulled into the church parking lot. Everything seemed quiet, normal. He had not turned on the outside lights. When he left for the hospital, it was long before dark. With little moon, the area around the church buildings could have been the inside of a coal mine. He turned the car in a circle, his headlights sweeping around the perimeter. He saw no one.

"Stay here, Sammie. I'm going to look inside."

"I'm coming with you."

"No. Stay here."

Father Frank got out and approached the church, trying to look around, but able to see little. He glanced at the sky. The moon was only a thin crescent, providing virtually no light. Given enough time, his eyes would adjust to the dark. He wasn't willing to give it that time. He reached for the handle on the door and gave a gentle pull. It opened. He tried to remember whether he had locked it or not. Yes, he had locked it. No, that was last night.

Didn't I have this same dilemma two nights ago? When I found B.D. in the church?

He ran through his activities just before going out to Ward's. He had supper, then went to the hospital, and from there to Ward's. He had not locked the door. Good, it means nothing that it's open.

He slipped inside. Instantly, the smell of diesel assailed his nose. He took three steps over to flip on the light.

Light filled the back of the church and a second later he heard Sammie yell.

"Look out, Father!"

The priest swiveled around and saw a long two-by-four barreling toward his head. Instinct combined with quick reflexes as Father Frank jumped, preventing a direct hit. But he felt the heavy board graze the side of his head and smash into his left shoulder. He crumpled to the floor. For Father Frank, the lights went out.

~ CHAPTER THIRTY ~

Ward pulled a lighter from his pocket.

"Stop!" Sammie yelled, his eyes like saucers. "You can't burn my church."

"Watch me."

And Ward touched the flame to the diesel he had poured on the floor. In an instant, the flames skipped along the diesel puddled along the vinyl tile between the rows of pews. Ward's eyes reflected the orange tongues of energy, and a sneer formed on his lips.

Sammie ran the few steps to Father Frank and began pulling on him.

"Help me, Ward. Help me pull him out."

"Sure, I'll help you."

He picked up the two-by-four he had used on Father Frank, swung it around and cracked Sammie on the side of the head. The teenager fell in a heap. He lay motionless. Even his chest did not appear to move.

"You two can pray together." He tossed the two-by-four down on top of Sammie.

Ward picked up the diesel can. He checked the fire. It wasn't burning as vigorously as he wanted. He swung the can back and started to throw more fuel on the blaze. But he stopped the can, poised in mid-swing.

Hold it. Remember what's important. This church isn't it. Get the next Baptist church and finish the job. Besides, the firemen can't handle two fires at once. Both of 'em will burn to the ground.

The diesel remaining in the can was all he had. He didn't have any more at the house either. The next church was the important one. It would complete his plan. Did he dare risk stopping by a service station and buying more diesel tonight? Maybe not. With two churches burning, police would be all over the gas stations. Someone just might remember him. So far, he'd been able to stay under the radar. A little bit of diesel from the carwash every day and nobody had a clue.

He looked back at the fire. The flames licked at the back pews. It wouldn't stop now. And nobody would notice until it was too late.

He glanced at Sammie. The scrawny kid looked like a popped balloon. *He ain't gonna cause any trouble now.* Ward shook his head. *He was a good friend. My only friend. But he'd gone soft. And the way he was talking, he might've gone to the police. It's the way it's gotta be.*

Ward looked at Father Frank. *He ain't moving. Probably dead already. The fire'll clean things up. No one's gonna figure anything out.*

He moved to the door, cracked it a few inches and peered out. No one in sight. He eased out and quickly shut the door. He stood as still as a post. Nothing moved. Even the pine needles on the trees were motionless. The sliver of moon hid behind a cloud. No security lights. He walked across the parking area at a normal pace and disappeared into the trees.

Now, to finish the night's work. Then the fires would stop. No more churches would burn. And no one would ever figure out why they started or why they stopped. The police will claim their increased patrols prevented any more. Good. Let them think that. Others will say it was a shame the guy got trapped in the fire.

In the dark, no one could see the smirk on Ward's face.

~ CHAPTER THIRTY-ONE ~

"What's this?" Mike speared a crisp white vegetable stick and held it up.

"That is Jicama," said Georgia.

"Okay. What is it?"

"I don't know. A Mexican vegetable. Good, isn't it?"

Mike popped it into his mouth. "Crunchy, anyway."

Georgia had prepared dinner, and had worried over how to arrange the dining room table. She finally decided on fresh flowers from her garden as the center piece, good dishes but not her best china, and stainless flatware. No candles. Nice but not too special. Warm but not too romantic.

A moment later, Mike held another item on his fork. "And this?"

"Mango. Adds a nice fruity flavor to the salad, don't you think," Georgia said, beaming her best smile across the table.

"Actually, it *is* good. I didn't think I liked mangos. But this is good." He continued eating the salad for a minute, then added, "I don't think I've had pecans in a garden salad before."

"Well, that's Texan all the way. Where were you raised?"

The main course consisted of pork chops, red cabbage, fresh asparagus and sautéed carrots. When they finished, Georgia suggested they have their dessert on the patio.

As they passed through the door, Mike leaned over and kissed her on the neck.

"Hey," she said. "It's still dinner time."

"I know."

"Well, I'm not on the menu."

"But you have on such an intriguing perfume," Mike said as he sat in a comfortable wicker chair. "It just drew me to you, sort of like a magnet."

"Probably the cinnamon," Georgia replied but the back of her neck still tingled from the brush of his lips, and she couldn't contain the smile bubbling up from within.

Thirty minutes later, they still sat talking about things that shaped their personalities, each wanting to know even little details about the other. No moon added to the romance that crackled in the air but Georgia's yard helped.

A small waterfall trickled into a goldfish pond that edged one side of the patio, providing an almost musical background. Roses and gardenias offered a heady scent. And somewhere near the back fence, a tiny bell tinkled so softly it was almost imagined rather than heard.

Georgia gave Mike a warm smile. She didn't want to ruin the evening. It had been simultaneously relaxed and exciting so far. But she had to bring it up. It worried her. Without a doubt, in the end, it held more importance for Mike.

"Tell me again, why you quit going to church?"

Mike squirmed in his chair, looked down for a moment as if studying the material of his pants, before focusing on Georgia.

"I used to go every Sunday." He chuckled softly. "Can you believe I used to be an altar boy?" The laugh ended abruptly and his tone became serious. "But after I joined the police, I began to see people, the world, more clearly. A great many of them were just plain bad."

"Many more are just plain good."

"Some are. Maybe most of those you come in contact with. But I see the general population. The drug dealers, cheats, child molesters, and thieves. People who abuse their spouses, or the elderly. The murderers. The line marches on and on. You can't see the end."

"Mike, you do *not* see the general population. You see, by and large, the worst side of humanity. Those misguided souls who, temporarily or permanently, have turned their back on God. It's not fair to extend that to everybody, or even the majority."

"Okay. Not the majority. But a goodly portion of the population."

Georgia leaned forward, closer to Mike, hoping she could make him look at things differently.

"I know people make mistakes. We all do. Some are worse than others. But the fact that we have a police department, laws, judges and juries, means that the majority of people are good, God-fearing people who want justice. Who want a better world to live in."

"I can't see that the church is helping at all." Mike shook his head. "Can you imagine how many people I pull in who go to church regularly? Who consider themselves Christians? In church on Sunday, abusing a wife on Monday. Are the churches doing any good?"

"Do we get a bad president, sometimes?"

Mike nodded.

"And sometimes, a bad administration?"

Again, he nodded.

"But you don't propose we do away with the democratic government, do you? Does that keep you from voting?"

"It keeps some people away from the polls."

"How about you?" she pushed.

"No. I vote. The only way we can change things for the better is to vote in good people."

"I admit there are people who go to church who don't follow God's wishes. But we don't throw out the system because of a few bad eggs. Some people consciously vote for a bad candidate, for one reason or another. Some of those candidates win. We don't abandon the system."

She gazed at the man sitting across from her, the man who had awakened feelings long dormant in her, a man who was becoming important to her.

"You haven't given up on society. You're still a policeman, trying to make this a better world. Don't give up on the church if everybody isn't perfect. The church helps, just like the justice system helps. Neither is perfect."

For several minutes, only the distant sound of a car intruded on the atmosphere of the patio. Finally, Georgia got up.

"I'm going to climb down from my soap box and fix us something to drink. I may have gotten too fired up."

~ Chapter Thirty-Two ~

Like rays of the sun slicing through fog, bouncing off each tiny droplet, magnifying it, and in turn being reflected, creating a spectrogram of red, yellow, orange, ocher and saffron, the fire moved slowly and deliberately. Here and there, it branched out looking for new matter to consume.

Father Frank could feel the heat from the purging fires of hell. He had failed. But why? Why was he trapped in hell? He hadn't revealed what he heard in the confessional. Had he been to blame for not getting B.D. to the hospital fast enough? No. His downfall was pride. He had tried to lead a good life but he let pride get the better of him, and pride was a sin. Could his transgressions have doomed him to the flames of hell?

Oh God, I'm sorry I've failed you.

He tried to turn away but fire greeted him. He moved, and an electric shock jolted his eyes open. He studied the flames. This was not hell. He lay in Prince of Peace Church. Slowly, his mind cleared. He remembered the smell of diesel fuel, Sammie yelling a warning, Ward knocking him down.

Fire was destroying God's church.

Father Frank tried to push himself up and pain stabbed through his shoulder and down his left arm. He tried to ignore it, but his left arm would not allow that. Groaning with the effort, he turned over. Holding his breath, he tried his right arm. It worked. He forced himself up.

The fire had not engulfed much of the church yet. Maybe he could stop it. Father Frank looked around for something he could use to beat out the flames. What he saw was a body.

He moved to the body and bent down. Sammie. Now Father Frank remembered. Sammie had yelled a warning, which probably saved the priest's life. It appeared Sammie had gotten the worst of it.

Father Frank put his hands under Sammie's arms and started to pull. The pain stopped him as effectively as a kick in the gut. He tried again, this time looping his right hand under Sammie's left arm. His first task was to turn the teenager around. Sammie was not a large boy but Father Frank was not his robust self. It took several tugs before he managed to swing the boy around.

The priest checked the fire. It was gaining momentum. He wiped the sweat off his brow, out of his eyes. His head throbbed. Even breathing was arduous. He had made little progress, and already he felt exhausted. He took two deep breaths, then, using his good arm, dragged Sammie toward the door.

Father Frank had never thought this area was large but as he labored to haul the unconscious teenager to safety, the door seemed a hundred feet away. Sammie gave no indication he was alive and as Father Frank stopped to catch his breath, he realized he had not checked Sammie's pulse or his breathing. He studied Sammie. If he was breathing, the priest could not tell.

"Come on, Sammie. Breathe."

With renewed effort, the priest pulled the boy toward safety, toward fresh air. Finally, he reached the door. He pushed it open with his hip. Immediately, the fire reacted, roaring with the new-found oxygen supply. Flames lashed out toward the two people between it and the source of air.

Father Frank looked at the flames, then at Sammie's inert body. With a surge of energy, the priest yanked Sammie through the door. He dropped Sammie's arm, stepped over him, and slammed the church door closed, shutting off the fresh incentive for the flames.

The priest dropped to his knees and felt for a pulse in Sammie's neck. The boy's heart still beat, but it was a weak effort.

Father Frank looked at the church and back at Sammie. "I can't carry you away. I've got to get help," he said to the still unconscious form. "I'll be right back."

The priest raced across the parking area to the rectory. Each jolt of his foot jarred his shoulder and shot pain down his arm. He swung his right arm across his chest to clamp his left arm against his side. Still, each step punished him.

Ignore it. Think about something else. No time to slow down.

His race across the parking lot felt like a marathon. Even the two steps up to the porch of the rectory were daunting. Inside the rectory, he ran to the phone, misdialed the first time, hitting an 8 instead of the 9. He pressed the switch hook and carefully punched in 9-1-1. He waited. It seemed like precious minutes were ticking by before anyone bothered to answer the phone.

"9-1-1. What is your emergency?"

"Fire. Prince of Peace Church is burning. On Vine Street." He caught his breath as he listened. "Father Frank DeLuca, the pastor." He listened again. "Someone is hurt. We need an ambulance. A boy is hurt. Unconscious. Please hurry." He looked back toward Sammie as he listened. "No, I can't stay on the line."

When Georgia returned with the drinks, she sat on a different piece of the wicker furniture, changing position and topic.

"What kind of movies do you like?" she asked.

"Action movies. Spy movies. And of course, the old westerns."

"I like all genres. But I can't abide the vulgar language so many of today's movies contain. Language is what sets us above the animals. Vulgar language lowers us back down."

"Spoken like an English teacher. I'll watch my tongue. Speaking of language, what do you call the piece of furniture you're sitting on?"

"It's a love seat."

"That's what I thought. So you should not be sitting on it alone." Mike got up from his chair and joined her. "I must admit, this is much better." He put his hand lightly on her shoulder.

"A shameless maneuver if I ever saw one," she said, with a tinkling laugh.

Georgia moved slightly to nestle closer to Mike. A tiny smile played on her lips as she thought about how easily she had slipped into the dating game. Her initial fears had proved unfounded. Mike had been so abrupt in meeting her, immediately asking her out and basically refusing to take no for an answer. But now, when she said no, such as when he wanted to come in the other night, he accepted it with grace. She was able to control her own destiny.

This time, his lips found the side of her neck and she tilted her head to give him greater access. It had been so long. She had forgotten how warm and comforting it was to have a man close. Not any man. The right man.

She turned and placed her mouth on his and felt her body react to his presence. Mike encircled her with his arms and drew her closer, bringing their bodies into more contact.

I'm losing my head, Georgia thought. *And I don't care.*

It had been a long time since her body had experienced this prickling sensation. She felt suddenly warmer. And hungry.

She pulled back, breathing rapidly. "I'm like someone in from a long stay in the desert. I need to drink slowly. I need to indulge myself carefully."

"We have a lot of time."

No sooner had Mike spoken than his cell phone intruded on their privacy.

"Oakley." He listened for a few seconds. "Okay. I'm on my way."

He snapped the phone closed and leaned away from Georgia. "I am truly sorry, but I've got to go."

"What is it?"

His jaw clenched and he looked directly into her eyes. "Another church fire."

"Where?"

"Prince of Peace."

Georgia's eyes widened in alarm and her mouth fell open. She suddenly found it difficult to breathe.

Mike stood, ready to leave. She jumped up. "I'll go with you."

"I don't know how this will go. It might be—."

"You're right. I'll take my car."

Before he could object, she dashed ahead of him into the house.

~ Chapter Thirty-Three ~

Father Frank turned on all the outside lights, then hurried back to watch over Sammie until the emergency medical team arrived.

The firemen arrived first. Almost before the trucks stopped, men were on the ground, pulling out hoses, hooking them up to the pump, stringing them out toward the church. The Fire Chief called out orders and moved among his men to direct the effort.

Only a minute behind, the ambulance raced into the parking lot, lights flashing, siren calling attention to a crisis. Father Frank stood up, yelling and waving frantically at the EMS, guiding them to Sammie.

Several cars with blue bubbles on the top arrived and volunteer firemen raced over to help the professionals. Yet another fire truck stopped on the road just down from the church parking lot, and attached a hose to a fire plug, tapping into a larger supply of water.

Two minutes later, three cars entered the parking lot. Detective Mike Oakley jumped out of the first. Georgia Peitz bounced from the second. Both headed toward the ambulance. The third car skidded to a stop and Officer Tom Turner stepped out.

Two EMTs worked on Sammie for a few minutes before loading him on a stretcher. At that moment, his eyes fluttered and opened. Father Frank was standing beside him. The boy's eyes were listless, apparently unable to focus on anything.

"You're going to be okay, Sammie. We're taking you to the hospital," said Father Frank.

Sammie's eyes squinted and took on the look of pain.

"Everything's going to be okay," Father Frank said, and prayed he was right.

Sammie tried to move his head, but the EMTs had fastened a brace around him to keep his head and neck immobile.

"No," the boy rasped.

"The firemen are here. They'll save Prince of Peace." Father Frank tried to give Sammie a reassuring smile.

Sammie tried again, his voice weak, no more than a ragged whisper. But his concern came through strong. "Burn ... 'nother ... church."

Mike now stood beside Father Frank. The EMTs tried to pick up the stretcher to move it into the ambulance. The detective restrained it with his hand.

"Another church? Tonight?" asked Mike.

"Yes." Sammie's eyes closed.

"We've got to take him to the hospital now," said one of the medical technicians.

Mike held up his finger. "One second." To Sammie, he asked, "Which church?"

Sammie opened his eyes into thin slits. They closed almost immediately.

Father Frank leaned close, touched the boy's cheek, and whispered, "Please, Sammie. Can you tell us which church Ward is going to burn?"

Again, the boy's eyelids opened mere millimeters, then collapsed. His breathing was labored.

This time, before either Father Frank or Mike could say anything else, the two EMTs picked up the stretcher and loaded it into the ambulance.

"If you care about this boy at all, we've got to get him to the hospital." They shut the door, got in the ambulance and drove off.

Father Frank, Mike, Georgia, and Officer Turner watched the flashing lights exit the parking lot. Over near the church hall, another car was parked, and a man stood some distance in front of it watching. Mike focused on him, and started to walk in his direction. As soon as Mike took his first step, the man turned to leave.

"Hold it. Pine Tree Police. Stop right where you are. Don't take another step."

The man hesitated, and in that time, Mike closed the distance.

Mike put his hand on the man's shoulder. "We need to talk about why you're always at these fires."

Earl turned. "Like hell we do."

He shoved Mike hard enough the detective, caught unaware, fell down. Earl headed for his car.

Turner rushed up beside Mike. "Shoot him," he yelled. "He assaulted a police officer. He's resisting arrest, probably burned all those churches. He's evading arrest. Shoot him."

From his position on the ground, Mike just winced as he looked up at Turner.

"Then I will. He's escaping." Tom unsnapped the safety strap, yanked out his revolver, raised it, and aimed it at Earl's back.

~ Chapter Thirty-Four ~

"Tom," Mike yelled.

Father Frank ran the last few feet and slammed Turner's hand just at the gun went off. The bullet buried itself in the parking lot.

"You're interfering with a police officer," Turner screamed. "Get out of my way."

Mike jumped to his feet and put his hand on Turner's arm. "Put that away. You don't shoot a man because he shoved me and walked away."

"He assaulted a police officer. He resisted arrest." Turner shrieked.

"Holster your piece, Officer," Mike commanded. "We'll talk about this later."

Officer Tom Turner, red-faced and breathing rapidly, reluctantly holstered his gun.

Earl's car door slammed. In seconds, the engine started and Earl drove away.

Mike watched the car leave. "Tom, go keep any spectators out of the firemen's way." His voice softened but the authority was still strong. "We'll catch Earl later."

Turner headed over to where the firemen were working.

Mike watched Tom for a moment, and then turned to Father Frank. "Thanks."

"For what?"

"For keeping Tom from making a *big* mistake. If you hadn't hit his arm, I think he would have shot Earl in the back. And regardless of what we find out about Earl, that would have been very, very bad for Tom."

"I'm just glad I got there in time," said Father Frank. "Right now, we need to go find Ward."

"Do you believe that boy? I mean, about another church fire tonight?"

Without hesitation, Father Frank nodded. "Yes, I do. And having encountered Ward tonight, I have no doubt."

"This Ward guy started the fire here?"

"Yes. I tried to stop him but couldn't," said the priest.

"How long ago did he leave?"

"I'm not sure. He knocked me out with a two-by-four. I don't think I was out very long. When I came to, the church was on fire." Father Frank shrugged. "I'm guessing. I don't think I was out more than a few minutes. Maybe he's been gone ten minutes. Maybe a little longer."

Mike rubbed both hands on his face, then through his hair. Thirty feet away, the firemen stood in the door, shooting water into the church. Mike pulled out his cell and pushed a button, even as he walked toward the church.

"This is Oakley. Connect me to Nelson. Priority one."

In a moment, Mike was talking again. "We may have another fire tonight. Church fire. I'll—." He listened for only a second. "Just take my word for it. I'll cover those on the west side. Get someone on the rest. We're looking for a Ward—." He looked at Father Frank.

"Campo. Nineteen, around five feet eleven, a hundred and seventy-five pounds. Probably has a diesel can."

"Campo." He repeated the description. "I don't know if he's armed but he is dangerous. Approach with caution."

He flipped the phone closed. Already, people were beginning to gather, some who had an emotional investment in the building, and others who always came out for a disaster, like the people who went to auto races just in case there was a crash.

Mike and Father Frank reached Tom and Georgia.

"Tom, stay here with the firemen. Probably nothing you can do but crowd control. Keep the people out of the way." Mike paused a second. His voice took on cold authority. "And keep your piece holstered." Then he started for his car.

"I'm coming with you," said Father Frank. "Nothing I can do here. The firemen don't want me in the way." He turned to Georgia. "Can you go to the hospital and check on Sammie?"

"Of course," she said with a nod. "But don't you need to go to the hospital yourself?"

"No. I'm fine. I'll go later."

Georgia nodded. "I'll call Mike if there's anything serious to report."

"Thanks, Georgia."

Father Frank took off at a jog to catch Mike, each step causing pain to shoot through his shoulder.

"Where do we start? There's probably thirty churches in Pine Tree." Mike backed the car around, gesturing for people to move out of the way.

"Start with the Baptist Churches," said Father Frank.

"Baptist?"

"Yes. The first three were all Baptist."

"But tonight, it was a Catholic Church." Mike turned into the street.

"I believe Prince of Peace was different. I think Ward was angry at me, maybe at Sammie. This is an exception."

Mike gave the priest a quizzical look.

"Mike, I don't know. And I don't have a real reason why. But my guts tell me Baptist." He waved his hand. "We have to start somewhere. It's my best guess. Have you got a better one?"

"Okay. I don't have a better suggestion." Mike stopped at the intersection. "Must be a dozen Baptist churches around Pine Tree."

"Eleven. But three have been burned. Only eight left," said Father Frank. "Turn right."

"Eight is enough."

"*If* he stays in close. There's probably another dozen within six or eight miles of town."

"Thanks." Mike sighed. "We'll cover town first." Another minute passed. "There's Elm Avenue Baptist."

"No fire."

"That we can see. We'd better check inside, see if he's still dousing it with diesel."

"I don't see a car," said Father Frank.

"Did you see one at Prince of Peace?"

"Good point."

Mike skidded the car to a stop. "I'll check around back. You check the front door. If it's open, do not go in. Wait for me."

A minute later, both men jumped back in the car. "What do you think? Pecan Grove or Third Street?"

Mike started the car.

"Pecan Grove."

He made a left turn. "Okay. What's your gut telling you?"

"It's a frame building. Third Street is brick. Won't burn as easily."

Mike gave a short chuckle. "Thinking like a criminal, I see."

They checked Pecan Grove Baptist Church. Nothing appeared to be out of the ordinary. Doors all locked. No windows broken. No smell of diesel. No sign of Ward's car. In less than a minute, they were on their way again.

"And what's the matter with your left arm?" Mike asked as they sped for the Third Street Baptist Church. "You seem to be favoring it. Actually, you look like you're in a lot of pain."

"I managed to get most of my head out of the way, but the two-by-four got me on the left shoulder. It hurts like the devil."

They turned a corner. The church stood at the end of the block.

"Look," Father Frank almost shouted.

A car was parked behind some bushes that flanked the parking lot of the Third Street Baptist Church. As they got closer, the dark car turned out to be a Chevy about ten years old. When he saw the smashed left rear fender, a tiny smile eased onto Father Frank's face.

"From what Sammie told me when we were driving to Prince of Peace tonight, that could be Ward's car."

Mike coasted to a stop near the car. He opened his door, got out, and slipped his service revolver out of its holster. Quietly, he approached the car, checking all around. He looked inside. No sign of Ward.

He got back in his car and eased into the church parking lot. "Wait here," said Mike.

"No."

"Then stay behind me, and out of the way. This man's probably killed one person already, and tried to kill you and Sammie. And, frankly, you don't look in any condition to fight."

Without further words, both men slipped out of the car, pushed the doors closed as quietly as possible, and started for the building. The moon was still just a sliver, and as they moved toward the church, even that slid behind a cloud.

A distant street light outlined the top of the building, only making the black asphalt area seem even darker. Somewhere in the distance, a TV broadcast a comedy show, and periodic laughter drifted along on the slight breeze.

The deep throaty sound of an eighteen-wheeler motor-braking as it entered town mingled with the TV sounds. All normal sounds. Nothing alarming.

Father Frank felt the hairs on the back of his neck stiffen.

As they reached the corner of the building, Father Frank veered off to the right. He knew there was a side door and headed for it. A narrow garden was planted between the walk and the building. Father Frank crept along. Suddenly, not two feet in front of him, something emerged from the garden.

Startled, he jumped back, almost tripping in the process. An armadillo backed out onto the sidewalk, turned and wandered off in search of a better place for a nighttime snack.

Father Frank could not believe how fast his heart was beating, or the tingling he felt in his arms.

A little on edge, aren't we? What will I do if a bat flies by? Or Ward comes out?

A moment later, he got to the side door. He reached out a tentative hand, hesitated, then tugged gently on the handle. To his dismay, the door opened.

He slipped inside and silently closed the door behind him. Immediately, the pungent odor of diesel assaulted his nostrils. He stood still, squinting, trying to make out shapes inside the darkened church. The emergency exit signs offered precious little light. High above, stained glass windows gave a hint of their colors but offered no illumination. He breathed in. The diesel was close. Which probably meant Ward was too.

The front door rattled, disturbing the silence. And when it did, Father Frank saw a shadow in front of him move ever so slightly. It was a person. Even in the darkness, Father Frank could see the shadow turn toward him, and then raise an arm.

"Ward, the police are here."

"Yeah. And the firemen'll be here soon as they give up on your church."

The click was accompanied by a flash of light.

Chapter Thirty-Five

Father Frank saw Ward in the wavering glow of a cigarette lighter. A sneer seemed to dance on his face as the flame fluttered.

"Guess you're tougher'n I thought. Figured you was dead." Ward started to stoop. "Maybe this time. You're standing on the diesel." The boy let out a short, sinister laugh.

"Wait." Father Frank had to keep Ward talking, not lighting a fire. "If I'm standing on the diesel, and you light it there, how do you get out?"

"Same way I got in. The door behind me. I ain't going out the door you come in. Didn't know it was open. So, let's get it on."

"Before you do that, can I ask you a question?"

"Ask away. Maybe I'll answer. Maybe not."

Father Frank waited, hoping Mike would hurry up. The priest turned his head slightly, held his breath, trying to hear any sound indicating Mike was on his way. What was he doing, anyway?

"Get on with it, Frank." The priest's name came out a sneer. "Clock's tickin'."

"Okay. Okay." *Slowly. Slowly.* "I'm guessing you set fire to Prince of Peace because it's my church, and you're mad at me."

Wait.

Wait.

"Maybe you're mad at Sammie, too. So, you decided to burn down Prince of Peace."

"Yeah, yeah. That ain't a question."

"I'm getting to the question." He coughed a little, trying to buy even a small amount of time. Maybe the lighter would run out of fuel.

"All the others, including this one of course, are Baptist churches." He raised his hand and ticked them off, as slowly as he thought he could get away with.

"Pine Valley Baptist Church. Calvert Road Baptist Church. New Beginnings—."

"I know the names. Get on with it."

"Why? Do you have something against Baptists? Did one of them do something to you and you're getting back at them? But then, that wouldn't explain four different churches. You see my dilemma?"

Ward started to answer. "You think I care—."

But the cavalry wasn't arriving, so Father Frank talked right over Ward's words.

"I mean, if it had just been two, a person might say it was a coincidence they were both Baptist. But four. That goes beyond coincidence, don't you think? I mean—."

Ward interrupted. "Got nothing against Baptists. There's just more of 'em around here. I wanted 'em all the same to confuse the police. Only one Catholic church in town. Couldn't do four of them. Same with Episcopalians. Only a couple of Methodists. See? If I wanted four of the same, had to be Baptist."

Ward started to stoop down again.

"Wait. Ward, the police know it's you. They're on their way here. They're not going to let you get away, fire or no fire."

"So, why not light it?"

"Because God will forgive you. Whatever you've done, He will forgive you. But you need to show Him you want to be forgiven. Not lighting this fire, not continuing down this sinful path, is a start."

Ward said nothing. He held the flame steady in front of him.

"With the authorities here on earth, it's over. But with God, it can be a beginning. Think about it, Ward."

Still Ward said nothing. Far behind the boy, a tiny sliver of light pierced the blackness. It was unable to reach Ward or

Father Frank. Mike was backlit, as was the revolver outstretched in front of him.

Very slowly, Father Frank moved his head from side to side, hoping Mike would see it.

"All you have to do is ask God to forgive you, and He will," the priest continued.

After a moment, Ward said, "You really believe He can forgive me? I've burned His churches. Killed a man. Don't see how He'll forgive me." Now, his tone was more questioning than argumentative.

"Others have done worse and been forgiven. God absolutely will forgive you, if you truly repent, ask Him for forgiveness, and—very important—change your ways, your life."

"In prison?"

"There are opportunities for good—or evil—everywhere. In church, in prison, everywhere."

By now, Mike had traversed half the distance to Ward, who apparently had not heard him. Ward flicked shut the lighter, plunging the place into darkness.

Mike snapped on his flashlight. "Put your hands on top of your head, Ward. Now."

Ward placed his hands on top of his head. At that, Father Frank walked over and took the flashlight from Mike and kept it shining on Ward. Mike pulled out plastic handcuffs and secured the arsonist's hands behind his back.

~ Chapter Thirty-Six ~

Immediately after Saturday morning Mass, Father Frank went to the police department. He prevailed on Mike to arrange a private meeting with Ward.

"I don't know why I'm doing this," grumbled Mike. "You're not his attorney. You're not even his minister."

"He doesn't have either one. So I'm filling in on the minister side. Besides, you owe me," said Father Frank.

"And just how do I owe you?"

"You did nothing on my slashed tires, and I introduced you to Georgia. And from what I'm sensing, you got the better deal, even if you eventually find the tire slasher."

They walked down to the cell block while they bantered back and forth.

"And if you had caught the arsonist earlier," continued the priest, "I wouldn't have a bum shoulder. What if this ruins my jump shot?"

The detective snorted. "You're right-handed. That's your left shoulder."

"Obviously not a basketball player. Your left hand helps bring the ball up for the shot."

"Obviously trying to pull the wool over my eyes. Bringing the ball up doesn't require the finesse of shooting. Your left hand will be able to handle that. If it ever could." Mike turned serious. "Why do you want to talk to Ward? He tried to burn down your church, tried to kill you and that boy."

"Sammie," said Father Frank.

"Sammie. By the way, how is Sammie?"

"Doctors aren't saying. And no one can get in to see him. I think he's still unconscious. I'll try again to see him, after I talk with Ward."

"In a coma?"

"I guess so."

"And why are you talking to Ward?"

They reached the door leading to the cell area. Mike stopped and waited for the answer.

"As you said, he doesn't have a minister. He needs one, now more than ever. Something happened to make him this angry. And I don't think Josephson was an accident. I think Ward knew him. You knew—" Father Frank stopped, not certain whether he should mention the Child Protective Services involvement.

When the priest didn't continue, Mike said, "We know Child Protective Services worked with Ward when he was ten years old."

"And his mother ran off and left him?"

"Yes."

"I'd like to know what set Ward off on this course."

"Whatever, it does not give him the right to burn churches or kill people," said the detective.

Father Frank ignored that. "Josephson was here in Pine Tree near the time Ward was with CPS. The records are sealed, but I did hear that Josephson was seeing Ward's mother."

"The fact remains, he burned the churches. And a man is dead. I'm not much on extenuating circumstances. Know what I mean?" Mike opened the door. "You can talk to him. I doubt you'll get much out of the kid. We haven't."

Father Frank sat on one end of the bunk. Ward sat on the other, his head down, his expression sullen. He would not look at the priest. For ten minutes, Father Frank had tried to get the boy to talk. He decided to try a more frontal approach.

"Joe Josephson's death wasn't an accident, was it?"

Still, Ward said nothing but he now looked at the priest.

"He was one of your mother's men friends, wasn't he?"

"Him and a lot of others."

Father Frank decided to gamble. "What did she say when you told her Josephson was abusing you?"

Ward's knees began to shake, then his hands. He clutched the mattress, closed his eyes as tears threatened to escape. Father Frank wanted to put his arms around the young man, offer some comfort, perhaps the first comfort he had ever received. But Father Frank didn't move.

"She didn't care." It came out as more hopeless than angry. After a minute, eyes still closed, he said just above a whisper. "She said I should ignore it, be nice to him."

Now, he imitated his mother's whinny voice. "'Be nice to Mister Josephson,' she said. 'I think he might marry me and we don't wanna make him mad. After we're married, I'll ask him to stop.'" Ward caught his breath. "That's what she said when I told her."

Ward shook with silent sobs. A few tears seeped out from his tightly closed lids.

After a while, he continued. "'Course he didn't. One day, he just didn't show up. Didn't come around again." He opened his eyes, now red and sad. "I was *happy*. No more ..." He looked directly at Father Frank.

"Mom got unhappy, then mad. She beat me, said it was my fault he left. My fault he didn't marry her. Every day, she would look at me like she hated me, like I was the cause of all her problems."

He laughed a mirthless laugh. "What a joke. *She* was the cause of all *my* problems. And he never was gonna marry her. None of 'em were. When she disappeared a year later, you think I cried? It was the best day of my life."

Ward looked at the floor and he was quiet.

"But Josephson came back?" prompted Father Frank.

"Yeah. But I was bigger then, and stronger. One look and he knew not to mess with me."

Ward's focus remained on the floor. The tears were gone now. The pain was not.

After a minute, Father Frank asked, "How did you get him into the New Beginning Baptist Church?"

Ward smirked. "Easy. Told him I had some pictures Mom had taken of me and him. I thought the police would like 'em. He suckered right in. Said he'd buy 'em from me. I said sure, for a couple hundred bucks. Come on out. I knew he wouldn't wanna do that. Afraid I'd set a trap. So I said, okay. How about a church? You know, what could be safer than a church? He said fine, but he needed a week to get the money." Ward looked at Father Frank.

"So, I started my plan and burned two churches." Once again, he focused on the floor.

For a few seconds, Ward smiled at the memory. "'Course, he got there early, planning to ambush me. But I expected that. I was there long before he got there."

Father Frank's mind raced down several paths, all disturbing. Finally, he said, "So you burned the other churches to cover up killing Josephson?"

"All but yours. I saw you as you were leaving my house Tuesday. And then Sammie starts crawfishing and talking crazy."

Ward looked at Father Frank and gestured with one hand. "See, if four Baptist churches got burned, and some sucker got caught in one, it had to look like an accident. After last night, I was through. No more fires. No more Josephson. I'd get my mind cleaned out."

For a long time, neither spoke, and Ward continued to stare at the floor.

Father Frank could not imagine the torture the boy had experienced. A ten-year-old boy, physically abused by his mother's lover, psychologically abused by his mother, and then abandoned by her. He never even knew who his father was.

In a more perfect world, Ward would have been in counseling from the time he was ten, maybe adopted by a family who would love him. Maybe he would have been able to overcome the memories, find life could be fair and warm and happy.

That hadn't happened. Now, Father Frank wondered how he could reach this troubled young man.

"Ward, you're in for a hard time. Five cases of arson, one case of homicide. You're going to need a lot of strength to survive. God can give you that strength, an inner strength to keep the world from collapsing in on you."

"You just told me that stuff last night to keep me talking, keep me from starting the fire."

Father Frank shook his head. "No. Not at all. Certainly I didn't want you to burn another church but I believed what I said. God will forgive you, if you ask."

"I don't think so." Ward hunched over even further, his chin almost on his chest.

"He can. And He will. All you have to do is tell Him you're sorry for all the bad things you've done. Convince Him you want to turn your life around. That you accept His love."

"Ain't nobody ever loved me. Nobody."

"God does. You are a child of God, and He's one parent who will never turn His back on you, never give up on you, never stop loving you." Father Frank could feel his stomach knot into a ball. The world had dealt this poor soul such a rotten hand.

"I've burned His churches."

"God has infinite power to forgive. But you must ask Him. You must tell Him you're sorry. You must mean it. That's all it takes."

Ward looked up at the priest. "I tried to burn *your* church. And I thought I'd killed you. How about that?"

"Ward, I forgive you. I truly do."

"I slashed all four of your tires."

For a moment, Father Frank just looked at Ward. "I've already forgiven whoever did that. So, I've forgiven you. But since you brought it up, why? What motivated you to slash my tires?"

"You was asking too many questions about the church fires. I wanted you busy doing something else, worrying about your car."

"How'd you know I was trying to figure out who was setting the fires?"

"I heard Harley talking about you." Ward looked at the priest and for the first time, his expression softened. "I'm sorry I cut your tires."

"Thank you. That's a good start. I know you've had a rough life, worse than I can even imagine. I doubt I could have done any better if I'd had such trouble."

He looked into Ward's eyes, hoping the boy could see he was sincere.

"If I can forgive you for banging me over the head with a two-by-four, slashing my tires, burning my church, God is capable of so much more. He can and *will* forgive all your wrongs." He leaned toward the boy. "Give Him a chance. Give yourself a chance. You need His help. He wants your love. He wants to forgive you."

The door opened and a jail guard came in. "Time to go, Reverend."

Father Frank got up. "Tell Him you're sorry. Ask Him to forgive you."

"Sammie make it out?"

"He's in the hospital. Not doing well."

Ward looked down at the floor. "Tell him I'm sorry. He's the only friend I had."

The priest started for the cell door, and the guard opened it.

"Father Frank," Ward said.

The priest turned to face the boy.

"Will you come see me again?"

Father Frank smiled. "You can count on it."

~ Chapter Thirty-Seven ~

Father Frank drove to City Park. He was encouraged by his talk with Ward. He might return to God. Father Frank thought about the life Ward had lived through. How could anyone expect him to be normal? It made the priest angry just thinking about it.

That didn't excuse the horrible crimes Ward had committed, but it did offer some insight. Father Frank believed steadfastly in God's willingness to forgive. God wouldn't give up on Ward and neither would Father Frank. A passage from the gospel of Matthew came to him.

"The stone that the builders rejected has become the cornerstone; by the Lord has this been done, and it is wonderful in our eyes."

Last night's events put an end to the church fires. Father Frank was convinced of that. What a relief that was for all the church-goers of Pine Tree. Actually, to everybody in Pine Tree. Misfortune for one part of the town damaged the entire town.

Thank you, God, for saving the two churches last night.

He pulled into the parking lot, parked and strolled over to watch the basketball for a while. So many unusual things had filled the past week that Father Frank had had little time for his basketball league. Fortunately, Dan Zimmerman had taken up the slack. The scores of the games and the standings were posted on the fence. The priest scanned the rankings. The realignment had worked. Every team had won some and lost some. No team dominated, none was a doormat.

Today, the Tigers and the Greyhounds were fighting like, well, like cats and dogs. Sweat and smiles abounded. Father Frank thought this contest illustrated what basketball should be—a fun game—hard fought but fun. Contrary to popular folklore, winning was not the only thing.

A boy on the sideline came over to him.

"Father, Earl has been around again. Not trying to sell us nothing. Just asking lots of questions. Trying to find out how things worked. We told him we didn't know and didn't wanna know."

Father Frank listened thoughtfully. "Thanks. I appreciate your telling me."

With the capture of Ward and the end of the church fires, he had put Earl out of his mind. But drugs still posed a problem for Pine Tree.

The priest continued to watch the game but his mind was not on basketball. What was Earl doing? Was he the big drug force in town, or just trying to get in? And why did he have to pick Pine Tree?

Thirty minutes later, Father Frank arrived at the hospital and went straight to Sammie's room. It was empty. Crisp sheets, tucked tightly all around gave no sign Sammie had ever been there. Father Frank's stomach suddenly felt like he was in a fast-falling elevator, and he clenched his fists as he hurried to the nurse's station.

The nurse concentrated on the computer monitor, not acknowledging his arrival.

"Hi. Can you tell me what has happened with Sammie Winters? He was in room two oh nine."

She continued to type, apparently ignoring him, or perhaps deaf.

"Sammie Winters. He was—"

She held up her hand. "Let me finish this entry."

She needed only a few seconds but to Father Frank, it drug on too long.

"The Winters boy?" She looked up. "He regained consciousness during the night. This morning, his doctor had him moved out of intensive care. Let me look up where they put him."

Relief flooded through Father Frank and he found himself smiling. Out of intensive care sounded like very good news.

When Father Frank finally found Sammie's room, the doctor was just leaving.

"Can I see him?" the priest asked.

"Yes. He asked about you. I told him you had a broken collar bone but were otherwise okay. He seemed relieved. You can visit with him for a few minutes, no more than ten. He needs to rest."

Over his shoulder as he left, the doctor said, "And so do you."

Sammie's eyes opened when the priest entered the room. He smiled, but Father Frank could tell the boy was still in pain. Two clear plastic bags fed liquids into a tube which ended with a needle inserted into Sammie's arm.

"Father. How's your shoulder?"

"About the same as your head. Sore. They've got a sort of X-bandage on my back to keep my shoulder from moving too much. It's actually the collarbone that broke but it isn't too bad. The doctor said it should heal with no complications."

"Doctor told me the worst was behind me. Might get to go home tomorrow."

"Don't rush it. Ward must have given you quite a whack on the head."

"Yeah. Doctor said if the corner of the board had hit me, it would have fractured my skull." The boy grinned. "Good thing I got a hard head, right?" He turned serious. "Dad said you pulled me out of the fire. Thanks." Again, he managed to coax a smile through his pain.

"Well, that wouldn't have happened if you hadn't yelled to warn me. You gave me just enough time to get my head out of the way." He laughed. "Of course, if I'd been as fast as I thought I was, he might have missed me altogether." His smile vanished and his tone became sober. "You saved both our lives."

"Thanks. Father." For a minute, Sammie looked like he was composing what he wanted to say. "Father, I'm sorry."

"For what?"

"If I'd told you more about what Ward was doing, he might not have burned Prince of Peace. Might not have broken your shoulder, uh, collarbone."

Father Frank nodded. "You're right. And if you had told the police earlier, several churches might have been saved. You should have spoken earlier. Keeping silent is not always the best policy."

"Ward made me swear I wouldn't tell anything. I thought we were friends."

"If your friends tell you to do something that's wrong, maybe they're not your friends."

"I know that now. I just thought... well, I don't know what I was thinking." Sammie looked on the verge of tears. "After the first one, it got even..." His voice faded and he looked away from the priest.

Father Frank laid his hand lightly on Sammie arm. "I understand. You start down a path, and sometimes it's hard to turn around. But you did. You stood up to him last night."

Sammie looked back at the priest.

Father Frank decided it had to be said and now was a good time. "You also know you have to tell Detective Oakley everything you know about the fires. Right?"

"Yeah. I do. And I will. Promise."

Sammie closed his eyes, and Father Frank could see he was still in pain. "I guess I'd better go and let you rest."

Sammie's eyes opened. "How's Prince of Peace?"

"Still standing. The floor in the vestibule and up the aisle a little is charred. And a few of the pews at the back. But the firemen snuffed it out pretty quickly. And the fire wasn't moving as fast as in other churches. The diesel didn't soak into the vinyl tile like it did in the wood floors. So a lot of the fire was just the diesel burning, not the floor. No doubt, we were blessed."

"And Ward only used half the diesel. He was saving the other half for another church. Did he burn down another church?"

"No. Thanks to you, we found him before he did. He'd poured the diesel on the floor and was ready to light it. You helped us get there in time."

"Thank the Lord for that," said Sammie.

"Yes, thank God for saving both churches. Well, I'd better go and see how the cleanup is progressing. There was still a lot of water in there when I left. Got to get that all dried out by tomorrow. Hang in there, Sammie. And sleep. That's the best thing."

"Ward's in jail?"

Father Frank nodded. "He said to tell you he was sorry."

"What's going to happen to him?"

Father Frank shook his head. "I honestly don't know. There are extenuating circumstances. But he did burn down three churches and killed a man. He's in serious trouble. He needs our prayers, Sammie."

CHAPTER THIRTY-EIGHT

Georgia and a passel of teenagers were scraping, sanding, and preparing the damaged pews in the back of the church. When the door opened, she looked back and saw Mike looking into the church.

"Come on in. Grab that rag over there, and help me wipe these down," she instructed Mike. She tried to sound business-like, but a ripple of warmth ran down her spine.

"I came to take you away from this, not to join in," the detective said.

Several of the kids looked up from their work. Mike smiled at them.

"Just kidding." To Georgia, he asked, "Why *are* you working on this tonight?"

"We've got some men coming any minute to stain and varnish the pews damaged in the fire. The kids agreed to have them all prepared. I'm the drill sergeant."

"Yeah, you look like a drill sergeant," said Mike. He chuckled.

"Okay. I'm the foreman, forewoman, taskmaster. Vic Lindale said if they get the pews varnished tonight, there's a fifty-fifty chance nobody will stick to them on Sunday."

The door opened and Norm Winters walked in.

Georgia looked over to see who had come in. "Hi, Norm. We're just about finished."

"Looks like your crew has done a good job." He glanced at Mike.

Georgia stopped wiping the back of a pew. "I don't think you two know each other. Norm, this is Detective Mike Oakley.

He's the one who solved the church fires. Mike, this is Norm Winters, Sam's father."

They shook hands. Deep lines creased Mike's forehead. "Sam? The Sammie who was hurt in the fire?"

Norm nodded. "Yes."

"He actually told us, as the EMS guys were putting him in the ambulance that another church was going to be burned. I didn't know whether to believe him but Father Frank was convinced." He looked at the floor for a moment, then back at Norm. "I need to talk to Sammie. Do you know why he thought another church was going to be burned?"

Norm shook his head. "No. He hasn't said anything like that to me or his mother. But, interestingly enough, he told me this afternoon he wanted to talk to you."

"Did he say what about?"

"He says he can add some information about the fires."

"The sooner the better. I can come to your house, if that's more convenient."

"Let me give you a call. He's still in the hospital. The doctor said he could come home tomorrow if all goes well today—on the condition he stays in bed and remains quiet. He has a pretty serious concussion. In fact, they ran an MRI. Thought for a while he might have a cracked skull."

"They've ruled that out?"

"Finally. Gave us quite a scare, though. He was out for, maybe six hours. Didn't respond to stimuli." He sighed. "His mother and I didn't sleep at all last night. When he finally came to, it was several more hours before he could remember anything about last night. He's still having severe headaches."

"Sam and Father Frank are our wounded heroes," said Georgia

"Yeah," said Mike. "Even with a broken collarbone, Father Frank managed to save another church from being torched. He's the one who really solved the church fires. And almost got himself killed doing it. All I did was arrest the arsonist."

"He sure did it the hard way," said Georgia. "He looked like he was in pain during Mass this morning."

"But he saved the church," said Norm.

Georgia looked at Norm, and could see the tired wrinkles under his eyes, the slight stoop to his shoulders.

"Norm, don't you think you should go home and get some sleep. You look beat. Or as Leo would say, you look like you've been pulling a mule uphill."

She glanced at Mike to see if he reacted to her mention of Leo. If he did, she couldn't tell.

"No, no. I need to help get Prince of Peace back in shape. I feel..."

"We're glad to have your help, Norm. But don't overdo it," said Georgia.

Norm smiled a tired smile. "A little stain, a little varnish and it'll look like new."

"How about some new tile on the floor?" Georgia asked.

"Next week." Norm looked at the detective. "I'll bet you've laid vinyl tile in your life."

"Well, I have, but it's –."

"Great. How about next Thursday? Seven o'clock?" A big grin spread across his tired face.

"I don't go to—."

"Thursday's fine," said Georgia. "I don't do tile. But I'll watch and tell you if you do anything wrong. Okay, Mike?"

The detective grinned. "I think I've been shanghaied." He nodded. "Thursday's fine."

"Great." Georgia beamed. "Norm, I'm leaving the kids with you. I think all they have to do is pick up the sandpaper and tools." She turned to the teenagers. "Guys, I'm leaving. Mister Winters is in charge. Any questions, just ask him. See you Thursday."

She grabbed Mike's arm and pulled him toward the door. "Let's escape while we can."

"Okay, where are we going? You said you were picking the place tonight," said Mike as he started the car and headed out of the parking lot.

"Bowling."

"Bowling?"

"That's right, bowling," said a grinning Georgia.

"Why bowling?"

"First of all, I like to bowl, and I haven't been in years. Second, I want to see how you react under pressure."

"Pressure?" Mike frowned.

"The pressure of losing to a woman."

"But I won't lose."

Georgia smiled and wiggled her head back and forth. "We'll see."

"And dinner?"

"At the bowling alley. They have good hamburgers, decent fries, and acceptable pie. What more could you want?"

"A thick steak?"

"Life is not always steaks, linen napkins, and waiters. Tonight, we rough it."

"And play under pressure," said Mike.

"Right."

"What if I win? How will *you* react if you're completely trounced?"

Georgia looked thoughtful. "That's a good question. I've never faced that before."

Both enjoyed the outing. Mike claimed that Georgia did a dance as she approached the foul line.

"I have never seen anybody roll a bowling ball that slowly. The first few frames, I really didn't think it would make it to the pins."

"Ah, but it did, and it knocked down a lot of pins," said Georgia smugly. "I, on the other hand, never saw anyone throw a ball so hard and knock down so few pins."

"When your ball got there, I think the pins just fell over from laughing. A lot of people throw a hook. But I've never seen anybody throw an 'S' before. How do you do that?"

"A trade secret."

Mike pulled the car into Georgia's driveway, turned off the engine and started to get out.

"Let's just sit here for a few minutes," Georgia said.

Mike settled back in the seat and waited. After a moment, Georgia began.

"I know you weren't that enthusiastic about the bowling, or the food but it really was fun, now wasn't it?"

"I had a great time. Even if you did nose me out on the last frame. With a ball that almost went in the gutter, yet somehow knocked down nine pins."

Georgia had been grinning. Now she turned serious. "Mike, I'm not a pushy person. And I certainly don't want to be pushy with you. But I wish you'd reconsider your position on the church."

He started to speak, but Georgia laid a finger across his lips.

"Of course, I'd like you to go to Prince of Peace because I do and I want you there with me. I know from our hours of conversations that you are a good person, and believe in Christian values. But I'm worried that you've let your work turn you into a pessimist.

"You see these bad people and you decide most people are bad. You see the failures of the church and you want to write off the church completely."

She scooted over and put her head on his shoulder. "I've been there. After Leo was killed, I was so disillusioned, so disheartened, I didn't want to believe in anything good. It took me a long time to get back to a normal view of life. If I really admit the truth, I don't think I actually made it back until I met you. Then I could see life was good and I could be a happy participant."

She stretched up and kissed him on the cheek. "Let me help you get a more balanced view of people and the world."

"A more balanced view?"

"Right. Only a few people are criminals. And I think churches should get some of the credit for keeping that number small. Are there some people who go to church on Sunday and break the law on Monday? Absolutely. Are there some policemen who capture a criminal on Tuesday and break the law on Wednesday? Yes. But you still believe the police department is worthwhile. So is the church."

She put her arms around him. His strong, muscular body felt good. More than good, it excited her, made her want more of him. This had all happened so fast, her first reaction was not to trust it. But she wasn't sixteen. She had learned to make a decent assessment of people. And, though she was frightened to admit it, she believed she was falling in love with this man.

Mike pulled her around and kissed her firmly on the mouth. She joined in, adding a fervor she hadn't enjoyed in many years. She felt flushed and thrilled. She was aware of the blood throbbing in her veins. She pressed her feverish body closer to the object of her longing.

When they finally broke apart, Mike took her face in his hands. "I don't want to lose you, Georgia."

"I don't think you can." She slid over near the door. "Right now, though, I need to go in and get my breath back. I'm not sure I'm in control of myself."

"I could come in, as a police officer," Mike said with a devilish grin. "Help you get yourself under control. I'm trained in that sort of thing."

"You can do a lot of things, Mike. But I don't think you're the one to help me control my emotions right now. If you came in, I might take advantage of you."

"I'm willing to take that chance."

"I'm not." She brushed her finger tips lightly across his cheek. "Not just yet."

They kissed once more at her front door and then, reluctantly, she closed the door on him.

~ CHAPTER THIRTY-NINE ~

On Sunday, Georgia sat on one of the freshly varnished pews. No one else, at least so far, had decided to try them out.

If I do stick to them, I'm not going to be happy. I should have worn old jeans, not this linen skirt.

Other seats were available but she was drawn to these that had been singed, had resisted the fire, and were now freshly stained and varnished. Perhaps she just wanted to welcome them back.

Now, Father Frank and two acolytes started up the aisle and the congregation started singing *Come Christians, Join to Sing*. Mike slipped into the pew beside Georgia. She looked up from the hymnal and did a double take, surprised and excited that he had come. She beamed as she handed him a hymnal. Her heart beat faster, and she silently thanked God.

Tuesday afternoon, Father Frank picked Sammie up and they drove to the police station. Sammie had made an appointment to see Detective Oakley and asked Father Frank if he would go with him to the meeting. The doctor had given Sammie clearance to go out of the house as long as he didn't do anything strenuous or jar his head. Father Frank suspected Sammie wanted some psychological support.

Dark clouds turned the day gloomy, threatening rain. Everybody in Pine Tree would be happy with the rain. Officially, they were locked in a drought. The pattern of the last month had been clouds, hot temperatures, high humidity, and no rain. Today looked as if it would follow that same pattern.

Sammie was quiet, eyes downcast, obviously not looking forward to his first day out of the house. Father Frank understood the boy's apprehension. He'd had information that could've stopped the fires. Three of them. Fear—or some displaced loyalty—had kept him quiet. But the moment of reckoning had come. No wonder Sammie was scared. But Father Frank respected the courage he was showing now.

The priest kept his comments to the weather, Sammie's recovery, and the basketball league. He avoided even mentioning the repairs to Prince of Peace, not wanting to bring the picture of that damage into the young man's mind. Sammie was already weighed down with guilt, and Father Frank anticipated Mike would pile on more.

At police headquarters, Mike offered water, coffee or sodas, and when both declined, he led them to an interrogation room. The sparse furniture consisted of an oblong grey metal table bolted to the floor and three grey metal chairs. Mike sat on one side. Sammie looked at his seat as if it were an electric chair. He hesitated, then sat down carefully. Once seated, he locked his gaze on the table top, refusing to look at the detective.

"Sammie, I'm going to record this so I won't get anything wrong, won't forget anything. Is that okay?"

Father Frank noted with relief that Mike's approach was kindly.

Sammie's eyes focused on the recorder. He did not respond.

Father Frank laid his hand on the boy's shoulder. "Sammie, Detective Oakley asked if you minded if he taped this session."

With what appeared to be a physical effort, Sammie pulled his gaze from the tape recorder and looked at Father Frank.

"Oh, yeah. That's okay."

Mike switched on the recorder, gave his name, the date, time and place, Sammie's and Father Frank's names, and the purpose of this meeting. He rewound the tape and played back what he had said.

He smiled at Sammie. "I always like to check that it's really working. Once, I went through a long session, only to find that the recorder hadn't captured a thing." He started the recorder again.

Father Frank watched without comment, his hand resting on the back of Sammie's chair, fingers lightly touching the boy, a subtle communication of encouragement and support. Mike appeared to be considerate of the boy's age, apparent distress and remorse. The priest could see Mike probing, trying to sift through the admissions and denials, the statements and answers, to find the truth—truth about what Sammie knew, when he knew it, and what part he had played in the arsons.

After thirty minutes of solid interrogation, Mike leaned back and asked Sammie if he wanted anything to drink.

"Yeah, a soda," Sammie responded. "Please."

Mike nodded. "I'll get you one. Father Frank, you want to go with me?"

"No. I'll wait here with Sammie."

But something in Mike's manner indicated that was not what the detective had in mind.

"On second thought, yes. I'll go see what your machine has to offer."

As they walked down the hall, Mike said, "Okay, how do you read him?"

Father Frank considered the question for a moment. "I think he is trying to tell the truth, as painful as it is. I believe he really didn't know much about either Ward's motivation or the details of how he carried them out. And I believe him when he says he was not present at any of the fires."

"Except Prince of Peace."

"Yes. And thank God he was there," said Father Frank.

"If he'd told us what he knew *after* fire number one, we probably could have prevented fires two, three, and four. *And* saved a life."

"Sammie knows that, and has to live with it. But I truly don't think he knew Ward's motive. I don't think Ward ever told Sammie about Josephson or the abuse. And I don't believe Sammie understood there was a plan to cover up Ward's revenge."

They stopped at the end of a short hall in front of a soft drink machine. Mike plugged in coins, punched a button and a drink popped out.

"Want one?"

"Dr Pepper, please."

The machine yielded a second drink, and the men headed back to the interrogation room.

"What has Ward said?" asked the priest.

"Not much. He's admitted to the fires. and the assault on you and Sammie. When we asked him about Josephson, he said "accident," and nothing more."

"Have you told him you know about the abuse?"

"Not yet. The district attorney wants to find the right time to spring that on him."

Father Frank popped open his soda and took a long pull. "I imagine he knows you know."

"Maybe. But the first time we actually bring it up will be significant. It's like when the other shoe drops. You know it's coming but you still jump when it hits."

"Does he have an attorney yet?"

"Yeah," said the detective. "Actually, he's got a pretty good one, not some greenhorn who barely knows his way to the bathroom."

They had reached the interrogation room when a commotion broke out in the reception area. Looking through a glass panel in the wall, they could see Officer Tom Turner and Earl pushing and shoving each other as they stumbled through the front door.

"You'll rot in jail for the rest of your life," Turner screamed. "Dora, he's got a gun. Shoot him!"

The dispatcher jumped up, her mouth open, eyes wide with surprise and fear. Her hand jerked to the butt of her pistol, and then froze there.

"Dora, *shoot* him before he shoots you," Tom yelled. "He's dangerous." He yelled louder. "Somebody. Help!"

Father Frank remained at the glass panel, unable to take his eyes off the scene, but Mike raced to the door leading to reception. Two other officers boiled out of the squad room.

Earl slammed Tom into a chair, as the two policemen burst into the room.

"He's got a gun. Shoot him," Tom shrieked. "He's attacking us."

He struggled to get up, but Earl shoved him back down into the chair.

The two patrolmen hesitated as Earl turned toward them.

"Shoot him," Tom screeched again.

Earl put up both hands, palms facing his attackers. The policemen grabbed his arms, pinning them behind the scruffy looking intruder's back. They shoved Earl face-down on the counter. Mike reached around and found the handcuffs on his belt. Roughly, he snapped the steel bracelets around Earl's wrists.

Mike searched Earl and removed a gun from a holster hidden in the center of his back beneath the dirty tee shirt. They turned Earl around and Mike found another gun concealed by Earl's shirt, tucked under his belt in the front. Mike looked at the gun, turned it over in his hand. He looked at Tom.

"That's mine," Tom pushed out of the chair. "He pulled a gun on me and disarmed me. Get these cuffs off me, and I'll take care of him. He's a murderer and a drug pusher."

It was only now that Father Frank realized that Tom Turner was in handcuffs. Mike fished in his pocket for a key and started to unlock the cuffs on Tom's wrists.

"Before you do anything foolish," Earl said, "I'd suggest you check my ID. It's in my front, left pocket."

He had a three-day beard, his appearance disheveled, his clothes dirty, and he had been treated roughly by the police. But Earl's voice was calm, not the angry, tough voice Father Frank had heard in the past. He didn't know what to make of this change in Earl.

"It's a trick," Tom howled. "And he's got a backup. Ankle hostler. He tried to kill me."

Mike ran his hands around Earl's ankles. On the inside of the left one, Mike found a small leather hostler with a Derringer tucked snugly inside. He inspected the gun, then handed it to one of the policemen who had helped subdue Earl. He stepped over to Tom.

"Check my ID first," said Earl. "Might help clear things up."

Mike, his face twisted in question as he looked at Earl and then Tom.

"Shoot him," Tom yelled. "Or get these cuffs off me and I'll take care of him. He's a murderer and a drug dealer. He attacked a police officer. He tried to kill me."

Father Frank watched in amazement. Twice he had heard Tom demand Mike shoot a person. Both times, the target was Earl. What was going on between Tom and Earl? And why, or how, was Officer Tom Turner in handcuffs?

Mike had the key inserted in the cuffs on Tom's wrists. For a brief instant, Mike looked through the glass window at Father Frank. Without turning the key, Mike pulled it out and stepped toward Earl.

"What are you doing?" demanded Tom. "You're not taking the side of a drug dealer over a fellow officer?"

"I'm not taking anybody's side."

He dug into Earl's pocket and pulled out a leather folder. He looked at the outside, and then glanced at Earl.

To Father Frank, Earl appeared totally at ease. Mike looked puzzled. And Tom looked frantic. Mike opened the folder and studied it for several seconds.

From where he stood, looking through the glass panel, Father Frank had a clear view of the leather folder. Inside was a circular badge. A five sided star formed the middle of a badge. Curved around the top was the word "TEXAS." Around the bottom, Father Frank read, "RANGERS."

Mike scowled at the burly man leaning against the counter, hands cuffed behind his back. "Texas Ranger?"

"Undercover," said Earl. "Looking for the bad apple."

"Don't listen to him. He's lying," screeched Tom. "Whatever he's got, he stole or bought with drug money."

"There's a reason why the drug dealers are always a step ahead of you," Earl said calmly. "Tom Turner. He tipped them off to all your plans. Your chief suspected something was wrong, a leak somewhere. Didn't know what or who, so he asked for help. Austin sent me here to find out where the leak was." He nodded toward Turner. "I found it."

"Don't believe him," Tom squealed. "Nobody said anything about a Ranger coming here."

"Even your Chief didn't know who or when. Had to be that way." Earl's manner was relaxed, confident.

"He's lying." But Tom had lost all bravado.

Father Frank sat in the interrogation room with Sammie, waiting for Mike to finish the processing of Officer Tom Turner. Earl hung around long enough to give a statement and hand over a collection of photographs, tapes, and notes he had retrieved from his Trans-Am. On his way out, he stopped by the interrogation room.

"Sorry I treated you so rough," Earl said. "But I had to play the bad guy. And when you stuck your nose in, well, knocking down the priest was a great qualifier for the bad guy."

"Apology accepted," said Father Frank. "What happened with B.D.?"

"Stupid kid couldn't stay away from drugs. OD'd or bad stuff. Beats me. I found him on the side of the road, looked like he crashed his motorbike. I knew right away he was in trouble. But again, I couldn't look like a good guy, taking him to the hospital. So, you got elected."

"What if I hadn't taken him in?"

Earl smiled, maybe the only time Father Frank had seen him smile. "Never doubted for a moment you would." The smile evaporated. "He still in a coma?"

"Yes. But the doctors are at least talking a little more optimistically."

"Well, I just wanted to say 'sorry' and hope there's no hard feelings."

"If you helped with the drug problem, it was well worth it." Father Frank walked over and shook hands with Earl.

Finally, Mike returned, looking exhausted. He lectured Sammie and said the information would go to the juvenile judge, who would decide what would happen after Sammie appeared.

"I'll suggest he assign you community service, no time in juvy. He may or may not take my recommendation."

Sammie sat, almost in tears, and didn't say a word.

"I trust you've learned a lesson from this."

Sammie looked up at the detective. "Yes sir. I have. And I appreciate your suggestion to the judge."

"Okay, you're free to go. Stay out of trouble. Next time, there'll be no question. You'll go to juvenile detention."

That night, Georgia walked into the Prince of Peace hall shortly before the POPsters began rehearsal. A dozen teenagers were gathered around the refreshment table, talking and laughing. Phyllis Traynor sat on the other side of the room, sorting through song books. Georgia walked over to her.

"Need any help?"

Phyllis jumped up from her chair, her eyes flashing, hands waving. "You won't believe what's happening on the benefit concert."

Georgia opened her mouth to speak, but Phyllis kept right on bubbling.

"Both banks are sponsoring the concert, along with Edward's Ford and Vic Lindale, and a bunch of others."

"That's—"

"And... and we're going for three performances. The kids have just about sold out the two we had scheduled, even with the higher ticket prices. Nobody's complaining about the price."

"Fantastic, Phyllis." Georgia managed to squeeze in two words.

Phyllis moved closer to Georgia and whispered. "With the sponsors, and ticket sales already in, we're over *twenty-two thousand dollars*. And we haven't talked to the milk plant or lots of other businesses. That's all in a week. And we've got two more weeks to go."

"You've been busy."

"Well, I've had a lot of help. Elliot Edwards is a member of Calvert Road Baptist. He was excited we were raising money to help the three churches, and *he* called Perry Hamlin at Pine Tree Savings. He goes to New Beginnings Baptist, really involved in the church. He came across big."

Phyllis sat down and pulled Georgia down into the chair beside her.

"So, I went to see Richard Howard at First National. I said, 'You're twice as big as Pine Tree Savings.' He got this little smile on his face and said he'd donate twice as much as Hamlin did. Everybody knows Hamlin is pretty tight fisted, so Howard felt safe. When I told him Hamlin contributed five thousand dollars, he turned pale and just stared at me.

"I wanted to say five thousand would be fine, that he didn't have to give twice as much. But I bit my tongue and didn't say a word, just smiled sweetly with my hands folded in my lap. Well, actually, they were clenched. After a minute, he reached into his desk, and pulled out a checkbook. While he was writing, he asked, 'Perry really donated that much?' And he handed me a check for ten thousand."

Phyllis looked like she might burst with joy.

"Good for you. And for Howard, too," said Georgia.

"I'm so excited, I can hardly sit still."

"I wouldn't have guessed."

"And the kids are really motivated."

"And best of all, they're learning the joy of helping others." Georgia snapped her fingers. "Oh, I brought a new member for the choir."

At that moment, Mike came through the door, looked around, and headed for Georgia.

Phyllis's mouth fell open. "Mike? Georgia, this is a teenage choir."

Georgia laughed. "Don't be silly. I'm keeping him for myself. But I talked with Sam—"

The door flew open and Sammie Winters walked in and sauntered over to the other teenagers. Hillary gave him a smile as bright as a harvest moon.

"I hear you guys need a really good bass," Sammie said, blushing.

~ END ~

Read an Excerpt from the next Father Frank Mystery

Over My Dead Body

By James R. Callan

It begins on the next page.

Also, look for the Sweet Adelines Mystery

Murder a Cappella

By James Callan and Diane Bailey

Murder a Cappella is set in the world of Sweet Adelines—a world-wide organization of women who sing barbershop harmony. It has the intrigue of the mystery, intertwined with the glitz and excitement of an international singing competition. Go behind the sequins to help Tina Overton, a member of the same chorus as the victims, solve these murders – before she is the next corpse.
Published by Wayside Press, 2012.

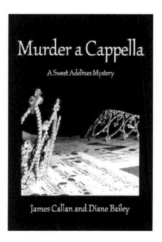

Over My Dead Body

Chapter 1

Syd snorted and thrust his chin toward his adversary. "Over my dead body."

The man almost smiled. "If you insist," he said easily.

Seventy-two year old Syd Cranzler squinted against the bright Texas October sun and scrutinized the well-dressed man in front of him. Syd was probably six inches shorter than the man, but Syd's voice had more iron in it. "Was that a threat?"

"No sir, Mr. Cranzler," Duke Heinz said.

Syd didn't like this city slicker, wouldn't have even if he weren't trying to steal Syd's homestead. Even Duke's clothes irritated him. The conservative black pinstriped suit, power-red tie and black wing-tips polished to perfection made the man look like he was posing for a magazine picture in New York City. And what was this "Duke" bit? Did he think he was John Wayne? "Why don't you just mosey on down the road a mile." He jerked his hand up and pointed. "Lots of land there."

They stood on pine needles under three towering trees. Forty feet behind them was Syd's small, frame house, looking like a giant, square tumbleweed.

Bud Wilcox, Pine Tree's City Manager took a step forward. "Syd, Pine Tree wants this shopping center *here*, inside the city limits. Think of all the tax revenue we'll get."

'Look, Pipsqueak, it ain't your house and land."

Bud reddened at the nickname Syd often used on him, but kept his mouth shut.

A mud-caked '92 Camaro rattled to a stop at the curb, and a man got out and started across the yard to where Syd was shaking his finger at Bud.

"So's you can waste even more than you do now? I ain't selling." Duke raised his hand and started to speak, but Syd cut him off. "And don't tell me again it's twice what it's worth. You don't know what it's worth to me. And what's this 'fee simple' bit?" He cocked his head to the side. "You think I'm simple? Take your money and go back to New Jersey."

Bud waggled his balding head. "It's a lot of dollars."

"He don't need your money," said the man from the Camaro. "He stole enough from me."

"Stay out of it, W.C.," Syd snapped. But his focus never left Duke. "You keep your money; I'll keep my land."

Duke spread his hands. "Mr. Cranzler, the Supreme Court says eminent domain can be used to obtain land needed for a project in the public interest."

"I know all 'bout the Supreme Court, and how they trampled all over people's property rights. I'd like to see some private company try to take the land *they* live on. They'd change their tune right fast. But that case was decided for a Yankee town. This is Texas. We still believe in property rights down here. And this ain't in the public interest. It's in Lockey Corporation's interest."

Duke smiled as he pulled a folded paper from the inside pocket of his coat. "Here's the court order, and it's signed by a judge right here in Texas." He held the paper out to Syd.

Syd ignored it. "Judge McFatage, right? He'd sign anything for a price."

Bud Wilcox leaned in. "Now, Syd, you shouldn't talk about the Honorable McFatage that way."

"Honorable, my foot. He's for sale. Common knowledge. You know what they say: he's the best judge money can buy. And it looks like Lockey's the buyer."

"Look, Mr. Cranzler," Duke said. "We're going to start dirt work in three weeks. I'd like to have all the paperwork in order by then. You've lost this fight. You might as well recognize that. You can delay signing. But by fighting this, you may end up getting less money and paying a lot of it to lawyers. You can't stop it. This project *will* be built. And it starts in three weeks."

"Three weeks?" Syd pulled on his chin and a little smile crept onto his leathery face. "I'm bettin' my lawyer'll have my appeal filed before then. And I'm thinkin' I can tie this up for years. You sure Lockey wants to wait that long?" His head bobbed up and down as he continued. "Be a lot faster to go somewheres else." Now he laughed. "Bet they're gonna cut you loose when this don't happen. Can your butt."

Duke's smile faded and his eyes turned hard. "Two months from now, this will all be asphalt."

"Like I said, over my dead body."

Duke put the paper back in his pocket. "Old man, you'll hardly make a bump in the pavement."

About The Author:

James R. Callan took a degree in English, intent on writing. When writing didn't support a family, he went to graduate school in mathematics, then pursued a career in mathematics and computer science. He has received grants from the National Science Foundation, NASA, and the Data Processing Management Association. He has been listed in *Who's Who in Computer Science*, and *Two Thousand Notable Americans*.

But writing was his first love. He has published a number of books and picked up some awards along the way. ***Cleansed by Fire*** is the first of the Father Frank mysteries.

Murder a Cappella, also published in 2012, is another mystery which Callan wrote with one of his daughters, Diane Bailey.

Callan lives with his wife in east Texas and Puerto Vallarta. They have four grown children and six grandchildren.

13796734R00126

Made in the USA
Charleston, SC
01 August 2012